JOY AMIDST TRIALS

Joy Amidst Trials

Jacian Thiessen

Jacian Thiessen

To my brother, Charles. You have been through so much, and yet you remain the kindest, calmest, and most loving brother I could ever have. You are a blessing and a gift to many. Keep on fighting strong. Let the peace and joy of God be your guide and constant companion through hardship, trials, and joyous occasions.

Introduction

I, Jacian Thiessen, purposed this book to portray that no matter how hard life can knock us down, we, in the power of the Joy of the Lord, can still get back up and face the next day with a smile in our hearts. For Joy is not dependent upon the circumstances of our surroundings, but on who we are within.

No matter who you are, you are never too young or too small, too old or too tall, too broken or too perfect, to serve the Lord Jesus Christ, and live a most joyous life!

Contents

1

Winter White Starvation

He was an only child. He had dark brown hair, which was always combed backward. His hazelnut eyes seemed to have darkened from their usual cheerful look. He once was the most energetic boy in the little town, despite the poor condition of his family. Food, clothing, and other supplies were normally close to running out, but they were always able to get what they needed when they needed it. Jeremy loved his life, his family, and his friends, nothing could take them away, or so he thought. For everything changed on that fateful day—September 23, 1816.

His parents had come down with a bad fever caused by starvation. Somehow, he was not affected. As he walked back home from his newspaper job, he thought of the awful morning about a month prior, after the newspaper boy came by.

As Jeremy went out to receive the newspaper for his dad, he looked around at the beautiful neighborhood he lived in. There were bright flowers around each house. Many of the fifteen houses that were in the village had a rustic cabin look. The village was surrounded by trees, with a single road running into it. It was a quiet remote village with the closest store located in another village a few miles away.

A few snow-covered trees were scattered about the village. The normally bright green grass lawns were now covered by a thin layer of gleaming snow. Neighborhood kids that had come out of their hibernating dens, had begun to play in the snow.

Once Jeremy had retrieved the newspaper, he turned around and headed into his own house, which was located at the beginning of the village. There was a tire swing that hung from the tree that was standing right beside the house. His house was partly surrounded by an old picket fence. As he walked onto the small porch, the boards underneath creaked with aching pain.

After Jeremy had come inside, he put the newspaper on the dining table near the door. His mom came from the cellar that was in the far-right corner. As Jeremy went to help her in the kitchen with breakfast, Jeremy's dad came downstairs.

After breakfast, as his father read the news, his always confident smile gave way to a worried frown. Jeremy remembered the following conversation perfectly, "Honey, what is wrong?" asked his mother.

Dad looked up and explained. "Remember that our country receives several of its supplies from Europe?"

"Oh, I remember, Dad!" exclaimed Jeremy.

"Well," continued Dad, "there is a war in Europe, which means that all supply lines coming from Europe are cut off. Food will be limited, among other things."

"But that means we could starve to death!" exclaimed Mom, as she ran to see what was stored in the cellar. She returned with a worried face and shared with us the sad news. "We have enough food to last us only a few weeks, and with the war, many of the closest stores and businesses will be closed!"

Now, about three weeks later, Jeremy reached home where his parents both lay in bed, extremely sick. He was the only one who kept them barely alive. Other neighbors had already died, and a few others were dying, just as his parents were. Life dragged by slowly. Many families had decided to move to larger towns, where more food was available.

One gloomy day, his mother said to him, "My son, oh how much you have grown in the past few weeks! You have made both your parents so proud. I love you so, so very much. I worry about what will become of you, but with the Lord's hope and peace, I know that you will be ok."

Jeremy brushed away the tears as he looked away. He couldn't understand why a so-called kind and loving Father would take the only family he had when he was just ten years old.

Jeremy's mom reached out her shaking hand and laid it on top of her son, "He loves you, too. He loves you so much. And He knows what is best for each and every one of us. I... LOVE... YOU... SON."

Jeremy tried to hold back the tears as much as he could, as he watched his mother fade away in the morning breeze. Later that day, when he realized that his father's time would soon come, he couldn't hold back the tears, "Are you leaving me, too, Father?"

A moment of silence followed. Only the broken sobs of friends, as well as Jeremy's, tore through the silence.

"Yes, Son. I must go as well. But fear not, my child. For though I leave this body, my soul will go with you, as will your mother's. But most importantly, the Lord Almighty will go with you. He will protect you. He will guide you through every step. Be of great courage Son, and fear not what lies ahead of you. For you are my son, my wonderful son."

Jeremy's father reached for his other hand and shakily took off a shiny ring. It had a green gem mounted on it. With a small fish swimming around it. "I want you to keep this, my son. As I have and my father did, and his father before him. I love you, my son."

Soon after his father passed away. It was near supper time, but Jeremy was far from hungry. All day, and all night, the young boy cried his heart out. No one could make him eat for the next few days. Even after the burial of both his parents, the boy did not move from his parents' bedside. He wished he could have gone with them.

Eventually, the boy went to live with some of his parent's friends, but the pain and the agony were too much to bear for the young man. He hardly ate, hardly slept, and hardly did anything except stay in his room. The family that he stayed with worried about him. They tried talking to him, but all of their efforts were in vain.

A month had passed by when Jeremy finally decided to leave the little town that held such a sorrowful memory. So, he gathered some of his belongings, and a little bit of food and water, and headed out to a port that was a few miles from his town.

After a few days, he reached the port just as the sun was going down. Suppertime. So, he went to look for a picnic spot. When he found one, he opened his bag, but to his dismay, there was nothing left. So, he decided to look for a place to sleep. He soon found a tree that had a branch shaped like a hammock. Once he was up in the tree, he fell asleep and dreamed of the big oceans. Jeremy wished he could sail the Seven Seas in the future.

To Jeremy, it felt like he had only slept an hour when the sun made its bright entrance, as it broke through the fog and clouds. Like a bear waking from hibernation, Jeremy got up and decided to eat, but then remembered that he didn't have any food left. He looked around and soon saw a little store. Having no money, he decided to steal some bread and a small container of milk.

He walked casually through the door, and as soon as the clerk wasn't looking, he quickly snatched some food and stuck it into his backpack. He turned around, and the clerk was still busy. He then quietly snuck outside, but just before he got out of sight, the clerk spied him and suspected that the boy had stolen something, for he acted suspiciously. "Hey, stop right there!"

Jeremy ran as fast as his little legs could go, not looking back to see where his pursuer was. But the clerk stayed by the door, figuring that the boy's parents might either be really ill or had already died. Either way, these were desperate times.

When he had run for what felt like a mile, Jeremy slowed down and looked behind him. No one was following him. He soon found a place to eat and sat down.

Soon, everything around him began to darken, which was awfully strange, as it was not even midday yet. He looked up and noticed that a storm was rolling in. He immediately started to think about shelter. He soon found himself knocking on doors asking for shelter. No one wanted him, nobody cared; this was proof to Jeremy that there was no hope or purpose for him. He started to cry, as he wished for his parents. He wanted a home. He wanted someone to love him and care for him. He could feel the strong wind and snow blowing against him, as he frantically searched for a warm place to stay.

2

Twice Saved

As far as Jeremy could see, all the houses were closed up. "It's . . . so . . . cold." Jeremy shivered. He felt himself falling onto the snow. He lay on the snow and felt like he was fading out of existence when he thought he saw a light coming from a doorway. He strained to see clearly, and as he did, he was convinced that the door was opened.

"I need... to get... inside..." Although only ten years old, Jeremy put up quite a fight against the undefeated wind. Jeremy was so close, and yet he was still so far away. As the snow dug into his unprotected face and hands, he collapsed on his stomach and slowly closed his eyes. However, just before he closed them, he thought he saw someone at the door. "Help!" he tried to cry out, but he was too weak—and the howling wind cried out even louder. He let his head lie down, thinking it would probably be the last time.

After the church had prayed together for one another, Pastor Jim asked the congregation, "Is there anyone who would like to share what God has spoken to them, or give their testimony, or perhaps what they want to do in the future? Now would be a great time."

After many had shared their stories, a young man named Junior, about fifteen years old, stood up, "I would like to someday save a life not only spiritual but also physical."

Immediately, an older man in his early forties stood up and said, "You know, boy, I think you will do just that one of these days." As soon as the church service was over, Junior decided that he would go see if there was anyone at the door. The members of the church always kept the door open during services. They did this just in case someone wanted to find shelter or needed help. Everybody was welcome here.

As soon as Junior reached the door, he thought he heard a faint cry for help. He tried to look around through the storm but didn't see anyone. Unsure of what he had heard, he started to turn around, but as he did, his eye caught a glint almost buried by all the snow. As he scanned the object, he noticed that it looked very much like a ring. Junior called for his father, "Dad, can you come here quickly?!" Junior shielded his face with his hands and his coat as he pushed out into the storm, toward the already-disappearing glimmer. Finally, he reached the spot where he thought he had seen the glimmer.

He started to brush the snow away from the spot when his father called out to him, "Junior! Junior! Where are you!"

"I'm over here!" he yelled back. He continued to brush at the snow until he finally touched the object. As he attempted to pull it out of the snow, he realized that it was fastened to something else in the snow. Not being able to see well in the storm, he reached down. It felt like a . . . a hand! "Dad, come quickly! I think there is someone buried in the snow here!"

Junior's dad, Mr. John Taylor, quickly got down on his knees beside Junior and helped brush off more snow from the boy's frozen body that was buried in the snow. Soon, Mr. Taylor was able to lift the boy out of the snow and carry him inside.

When others saw the boy in their brother's arms, they ran to get several thick blankets and made sure that the fireplace was nice and hot. As soon as they had wrapped the boy in the blankets and placed him near the fire, Mr. Taylor looked down at his son, who sat watchful over the boy, "Good job young man; without you, this boy may not have survived, but I think he will be just fine. How did you come across him?"

"It was the glint of his ring."

"What kind of palace is this?" asked Jeremy.

"Well kid, this isn't a palace. You see, you're in my house," said Junior, "You've been asleep for a whole month."

"How did I get here?" asked Jeremy.

"How about I tell you that another day, sound good?" Junior asked, "Right now, you can get dressed and come to the table for some delicious breakfast. See you there."

"Get dressed?" wondered Jeremy. He looked beside him, and there, on a small table, he saw perfect clothes; not clothes that were torn and stained for life, but clean clothes.

After Jeremy was dressed, he decided to go and look for the kitchen. "Too bad that boy didn't give me any directions. I mean this place is huge," thought Jeremy.

As he passed by the walls, he read many of the words that were on the walls. One that especially caught his eye read, "' Put on the belt of TRUTH, the breastplate of RIGHTEOUSNESS, the shoes fitted with the readiness of the gospel of PEACE, the helmet of SALVATION, the shield of FAITH, and wield the sword of the SPIRIT.' What does that mean?" he wondered.

Eventually, he found the kitchen. As he appeared around the corner, he saw the boy and what seemed to be his brother, sister, and parents. The kind mother looked up and hushed the rest of the family. She walked over to him and asked, "Are you hungry, my dear?"

"Yes, ma'am," he replied shyly. Not yet knowing quite where he was. *"Maybe it's the heaven that Mom and Dad talked about."*

"Well, you come sit over here, beside Junior. Don't worry, no one will bite you. May I ask what your name is?"

"My name is, Jeremy,"

As he was eating, the boy that had been beside him when he woke up, introduced his family. "My name is Junior, and I'm fifteen. My brother, here beside me, is Earl, and he turned thirteen two weeks ago. My little sister's name is Kiley, and she is eleven. These are my parents. We are the Taylor Family."

"So, what's your surname?" asked Earl.

"I don't remember. I guess it's all frozen in my brain," Jeremy replied.

"Come on, I'm sure you can remember your surname. Your surname is like the most important thing to remember in the whole world!" Earl answered back.

"That's enough, Earl!" exclaimed Kiley, "Leave the poor boy alone. Don't worry about him, Jeremy, he likes to annoy people, especially ones that are younger than himself." Then she whispered to Jeremy as she sat on his left, "I got him all taken care of, so you don't have to worry at all."

After breakfast, Mr. and Mrs. Taylor went with Earl to their garden for more vegetables and to the market for more clothes for their new guest, while Kiley and Junior showed Jeremy the house and neighborhood.

"Wow, your house is huge! Why do you need all this room, and what are these things on the walls?" asked Jeremy.

"Well, we let families that need a place to stay for a while come here; if someone is caught in a storm, or their shelter is destroyed by a storm or fire, they can also come and stay here for a while," answered Kiley who loved to answer questions before her brothers. Though she was only eleven, she was already proving to be a very beautiful and diligent young woman. Her straight chestnut hair came down to her shoulders. She was one who was always hard-working and loving. She loved to help her mother in the kitchen. Her mother often spoke of how great her cooking had become.

"There must be a lot of people coming in when a storm hits. You still haven't answered my other question, the one about the walls." Jeremy prompted.

This time, Junior beat his sister to answering the question, "Well, Jeremy, our parents put them up there so that people can be comforted, reminded, and also gain wisdom."

"What do you mean?" asked Jeremy.

"Well, how about I try and explain one to you? Do you have one in particular that you would like me to explain?" Junior asked.

"Yes. This one, with the armor of God written on it."

Well, that one comes from the book of Ephesians, chapter six. . ."

"Ephesians?" interrupted Jeremy, "I never heard of it. Are you sure that's a book? It sounds like a weird name if it is one. I thought the titles of books were supposed to be simple and easy to understand."

"Well, actually, Ephesians is part of another book, the Bible. Have you ever heard about it?"

"No... actually, yes; my parents often spoke of the book, before... before they died," said Jeremy, his voice almost a whisper. Tears ran down his cheeks as he began to miss his parents.

Junior and Kiley were both shocked to hear the news of Jeremy's parents. They had thought Jeremy had just run away, as many other boys had, and found their way to their house before heading back.

Junior asked Jeremy if he wanted to be alone for a while. He nodded his head, so Junior and Kiley left the boy alone and went to talk to their parents when they came home.

As Jeremy walked down the halls of the giant mansion, he remembered all of his short life, the good times and the bad. His whole life seemed to pass by him.

He had so many questions, like *why did his parents have to die so soon? Why was he still alive? What purpose did he have in his life now that he didn't have any family or home? How was he going to survive the rest of his life, if he was going to have to leave this place? And why would God, if there was even such a being... why would He take his parents away?*

Jeremy had been reading many of the phrases and quotes that hung on the walls, some he understood, and others he didn't. He had read and heard from his parents that there was a God of some sort, who lived in a place called Heaven, and that He was, one day, going to come and take all of the people that were His followers to His beautiful home. To Jeremy, it sounded like it was a place that only the best deserved to go. He knew he had done too many bad things to be able to go to such a place.

He continued to walk through the giant halls until he came to another writing. This one was long, and he thought about skipping it, but a word caught his eye, "deserve." So, he stopped and read it, and what he read amazed him.

"Jesus, the Son of God, did not deserve to be treated the way He was, but He was treated cruelly and died on the cross for your sins. He did this so that you did not have to die for eternity but so that you could live with Him in Heaven for eternity," he read. The thought of living in Heaven, forever, thrilled Jeremy, for he had been told by his late parents that they would go to heaven when they died, so he went to ask Junior more about this.

He searched and searched, but the house was so huge that he realized he was probably lost and was about to yell for help when he saw Junior's dad just down the hall, so decided to ask him what the writing on the wall meant and if it was really true.

"Well, of course, it is true, Jeremy. If it weren't, I would take it off the wall and burn it. But it's true, as true as true can be. Do you want me to explain it to you?"

"Yes, please."

"Well, first of all, I know it might sound absurd, but Jesus, the Son of God, came down and became man. You see, God sent His Son down to Earth as a sacrifice for people's sins. He did this because He knew that people needed someone they could relate to, and they also needed salvation. He knew that this would be the best way to have a relationship with His people, and that's what He wants—He wants a relationship with us, that's all.

Junior heard Jeremy talking with his dad as he passed by and came over to join the conversation. "In order to bring salvation to people," said Junior, "He decided that His Son would be sacrificed as a lamb for the sins of every person in the world and all those that would be born in the future. So, Jesus was mocked, beaten, and crucified, which means nailed to a cross, and left to die. But do you know what? He rose from the dead three days later! You see, Jesus didn't just die and rise from the dead, He took all of the sins of the world, every single sin that man would ever commit, and He carried them to the cross with Him. Those sins died with Him, but they didn't rise again.

"And so now, we as humans, are able to confess our sins to Christ, and He forgives us for those sins; He forgets that we have ever done them at all. It doesn't matter how many bad things you've done, or how bad they were, Jesus is always ready to take those sins away, and He is always ready to catch us when we fall. Does that make sense?"

"I think so. Where did you all learn this?"

"I've read it in my Bible. There, it tells the whole story of Jesus as a human being, from His birth to His death and resurrection. If you want, I can read you the story from the Bible today sometime."

"I think I would enjoy that very much. Now, could you point me in the direction of the kitchen? I think I got lost."

For Jeremy, the day sped away quickly. He was having so much fun with his new-found friends, he didn't ever want it to stop. He played all kinds of games, both inside and outside. He met many of the Taylor's neighbors, some of whom had come to visit to see how Jeremy was doing since the time of his discovery in the snow.

Jeremy also learned so much more from the Bible, as Mr. Taylor and his family read different parts of Jesus' life. That day, he learned something new from each individual. From Earl, he learned how to tease people in a way that he had either not known about or had forgotten. Kiley insisted on teaching him a little bit of everything that she had been learning from school, it didn't matter what it was. Junior showed Jeremy how to set traps for raccoons, rats, and other pests that liked to visit their farm and garden. Mrs. Taylor showed Jeremy how to prepare fish, and Mr. Taylor continued to explain many of the writings on the wall and in the Bible.

All too quickly, nighttime came around and it was time for bed. After everyone had given Jeremy their "goodnight hugs," he prepared to sleep and then shut off the lights. Just before he climbed into bed, he noticed how bright it was outside. As he looked out his window, he saw the full moon and all of the stars surrounding it. It was then that he remembered all that he had learned of Jesus that day. He felt a sudden nudge to ask Jesus to become His Savior. So, after some time passed, he finally got down on his knees and prayed the prayer of a sinner.

"Dear, Lord, I am sorry for sinning against you, Jesus. I know that you died on the cross for my sins. You died so that I could live. And so, I ask that you forgive me of my sins and come into my heart. Amen."

There was rejoicing in Heaven that night as another soul found its way to the Creator and invited Jesus to be in his heart. Jeremy also felt super joyful and at peace as he went to sleep, and he had a truly peaceful sleep—the best he'd had in a really, really long time.

3

A New Home

The days went by, as the Taylor family wondered what they would do with the boy. Surely, he had family back home, wherever that was. But as hard as they searched, they couldn't find anyone that wanted to take the small boy in. Many of his relatives had already died from lack of food or sickness, and those that were still around, did not want to take him in.

One early morning, Mr. and Mrs. Taylor awakened to discuss what they were to do about Jeremy. They had been praying for about an hour when Junior came out to the garden, where the two were seated. He knew immediately what they were doing and suggested something, "Why doesn't he just stay with us? I mean, we're all having so much fun together, and I think he really enjoys it here."

"We have been thinking of that too," responded his mother, "but along with another to add to the family, comes the need for more money, food, and clothing. We will definitely continue to pray about it. Now, go and wake up the rest. We will have breakfast going in a short while."

As Junior left, the couple looked at each other, and it was at that moment, they decided what they would do with the boy. It was like God put a thought in their minds at the exact same time.

Just before breakfast time, as Jeremy went to get something from his room, Mr. and Mrs. Taylor announced to their children what their plan was, and they all agreed that it was probably the best thing to do for them and for Jeremy.

At breakfast, Jeremy noticed that everybody was extremely quiet. Kiley and Earl couldn't stop giggling at each other, while Junior kept smiling as he looked from his parents and then back to Jeremy.

Soon, he'd had just about enough of this mystery and called out, "Would somebody please tell me what's going on here?"

"Well," started Mr. Taylor, "we have a really important question for you. Now, it's a real big one, and it might shock you so much that you won't finish your breakfast."

"Wow! That really must be a big question, but I won't be able to eat anyway if you all keep acting the way you are. So, it's your decision—stop acting weird or ask me the question."

"Well, in that case, we will ask you the question because I don't think we will be able to drop this whole thing and let you eat peacefully."

Silence filled the room for a bit until it was broken by Mrs. Taylor. "Jeremy, we, as a family, are wondering whether or not you would like to join this family and be a brother to Junior, Earl, and Kiley, as well as be our son?"

The thought of having a family once again shocked Jeremy. He remained speechless, his jaw had dropped to the floor, his head was fixed in place, and his eyes were frozen. He stared at the family, trying to gather himself together to reply, but he just couldn't. Finally, after a few more seconds, which felt like minutes for him, he blurted out, "I'd love to! Oh! This is the greatest day of my life!"

"Whoa, but it's hardly morning, yet. Don't tell me the day has already passed, I don't want to go back to sleep," teased Earl.

"Oh, Earl!"

Laughter encompassed the newly enlarged family. Jeremy was in awe of how the Lord had brought His perfect plan to pass. Jeremy felt overwhelming joy and peace. Peace that he would live a wonderful life, and joy that he could spend it with a family that loved him, both on Earth and in Heaven.

4

Unstoppable Joy

A few years passed by. Jeremy was fifteen and still having the best time of his life with his family. Although he had many friends from church, none were as much fun to be around as his oldest brother, Junior.

Junior, who was now twenty, still took plenty of time with Jeremy. Even though he had to go to work every day from 8:00 in the morning to about 6:00 in the evening, Junior spent as much time as he could with his family and his fiancée, Ms. Jessica Hope.

Jeremy clearly remembered the day that changed everything, twenty-seven months ago. He and Junior were enjoying another summer morning walk around the park a few miles from home. "I don't know how God could make such a beautiful Creation. Everywhere I look as I do schoolwork at home, out on the front lawn, I just see beauty. What do you think, Junior?"

"I would have to agree, I don't think there is anything more beau… be…," Junior stared at something walking on the other side of the park.

"Junior, Junior," Jeremy snapped his fingers in front of Junior's eyes, "Junior!"

"You were saying?"

"Oh, right… uh… uh…, I think I forgot."

"I believe you were going to say that 'there is nothing more beautiful than…'," Jeremy gestured to Junior to continue, but Junior was completely blank. Jeremy wondered what happened to Junior as they walked back home. Even at the dinner table, Junior was unusually quiet. His dad came quietly and asked Jeremy, as they were clearing the table, what happened to Junior that he was quiet and absent-minded.

"I don't know, but I'm going to find out," whispered Jeremy. He was going to go talk to Junior as soon as he had finished helping his parents clean the kitchen but then decided, instead, to first take a quick detour around the garden. It was so peaceful and quiet that Jeremy quickly forgot about everything else and just sat on a bench in silence.

"Jeremy?"

Startled, Jeremy looked around for the source, and he found Junior sitting right next to him. "Where did you come from?!"

"Doesn't matter, I've been looking all over for you."

"Me?"

"I have to tell you something."

"Are you going to tell me why you froze at the park?"

"It wasn't that obvious, was it?"

"Well, considering that you literally just stood completely frozen staring at something in the distance, yeah, I would say it was very obvious." But anyway, you were saying."

"Well, you see I… uh… I saw something, someone actually. And the person was a … a woman. And to be honest, if I am correct, she is the same one I've had a crush on since like the ninth grade. But I thought she moved away."

"Well, looks like she's back. What are you gonna do about it?"

"Well, I don't know."

"You can't just not know. Are you going to catch her, or not? I mean, I like life just how it is now, without any girls in the picture, but I suggest you pray about it. At least then you wouldn't be able to say, 'I don't know.'"

"Okay. If you say so."

So, Junior went back inside with a lot of questions, and a lot of mixed feelings and emotions. Jeremy also had some things to think about.

What was going to happen if God told Junior to chase after 'her'? What effect would it have on the relationship between me and Junior? I mean we always knew the day was going to come, but I guess I never thought it would be now. One thing is for sure, I need to support Junior at this time, more than ever; it doesn't matter how I feel now.

A week passed, and it was on this day, Friday, July 16, 1819, that Junior decided to confront the young lady, whose name Junior finally was able to remember after going through some previous digging into his high school life. Her name was Jessica Hope. Junior had thought through every possible outcome of him talking to Jessica. He shook from head to toe, which became very evident to Jeremy. So, Jeremy came up with a plan. "Junior, I think we should go fishing, instead."

"No, I can do it."

"Junior, I insist; because if she is the one and only, she can wait 'till after we finish fishing. Come on, get changed, again, and let's go fishing."

"Yeah, you're probably right. We haven't gone fishing in a long time. And besides, I'm way too nervous right now, and I only want to introduce myself. Just imagine when I'm actually going to ask her out!"

"Don't worry about the future. Remember, tomorrow will worry about itself. Come on, fishing clears everything out of the mind because you have to be quiet and patient."

So, the two grabbed their fishing gear and headed out. Their dad asked, "Where do you think you're heading off to?"

"Dad, do you see what we're wearing?" asked Junior. We're going fishing."

"And we are going to catch the prettiest fish that Junior has ever caught."

"What about the biggest?"

"That one is mine."

As the two walked out, Jeremy turned his head, and winked at his dad, causing him to be immediately confused, thinking to himself *"What mischievous things are those two up to? Oh well, I guess I will hear about it soon enough."*

Junior followed his brother to the "perfect" fishing spot. He was at first doubtful but then decided that it was just his brother trying his best to get him to think of something else, besides Jessica Hope.

After half an hour of fishing and almost complete silence, Jeremy spoke up, "You know I can see God being a fisherman."

"What do you mean?"

"Well, he knows exactly what he needs to put on his hook to catch just the fish he wants. He knows where to fish too. Now, we as people are like those really smart and suspicious-of-everything kinds of fish. You know?"

"Yeah, I think so. You mean that we are very cautious about whether or not we should take a bite. Sometimes, we are straight-up stupid too, thinking that we know what's good and what's not. I mean, we sometimes decide to eat garbage instead of taking a bite off the hook."

"But God is patient, and when he does catch that fish, he puts it in his own personal ocean of love, where He can always watch over his prized possession."

"Yeah, He is Love," Junior let out a big sigh and lay back on the pier. Then he noticed something, "Jeremy, why do you have a third fishing pole?"

"Well, I thought that..."

"Good morning."

Junior's heart stopped for he knew who it was, and quickly looked toward Jeremy for help. Jeremy smiled and replied back, "Well, good morning. How do you do?"

"I'm doing good, thanks for asking. Have you caught any fish yet?" asked Jessica.

"No, it's not the best fishing spot."

"Well, why don't you find a new spot?"

"Because this one is very quiet; the perfect place to talk."

"Well, I hope I'm not interrupting. It's just that this is usually the spot I come to when I want to reflect on what God has done for me."

"Well, if you want, you can grab that fishing pole and help us out. My brother, Junior here, is planning on catching the prettiest fish, but not having much luck yet."

"I don't know much about fishing, but I will try my best."

Junior showed a quick panicked look toward Jeremy. He wanted to shout at Jeremy, but knowing the situation that he was now stuck in, he bit his lip and kept his mouth shut.

Jessica sat down on the other side of Jeremy, who didn't know that he could have this much fun with his brother.

After a short moment of silence, Jessica spoke out, "How wonderful God's Creation is, the sky, the water, the animals, nature, and all of life."

Just then, Jeremy's line grew tight. "I got a fish!" he yelled as he pulled with all his might.

"It must be a pretty big one, here let me help you, bro. Ready? Puuulll."

The tug of war stood still for a second before a fish jumped out of the water and was pulled ashore. Everyone was awestruck as they looked at the fish.

Well, I did say I was going to catch the biggest fish, and I have even though it is only three inches long."

"Why did it take the two of you to pull in the tiny fish?! Do you think the lure was caught on something?"

"Not sure. Maybe it was God just saying that we need to stop fishing here," replied Junior.

"Yeah, maybe He knows that only suspicious fish live here."

"Suspicious fish?" asked Jessica.

"Jeremy and I were just having a discussion about God being a pro-fisherman. You see.."

As Junior and Jessica continued to talk, Jeremy excused himself and went back home. When he came through the door, he had the biggest smile on his face.

"So, are you going to tell me what you were doing today? And where is Junior?'

"Let's just say that Junior caught the prettiest fish in the ocean."

As the weeks and months went by, Junior and Jessica drew closer and closer, which meant less time with Jeremy. Even though Jeremy was a little fearful that Jessica was going to replace him, he still tried to help Junior as much as possible, whether it was mentally or physically.

One day, in the winter, Junior and Jeremy went on a stroll through their neighborhood. They soon walked past the church building, where Junior stopped and looked down at the snow in front of the doorway, tears began to glide down his face. "Do you remember this, Jeremy? I honestly don't know how you were able to survive being almost completely frozen, starving, and having traveled so far; I wonder how you never decided to just give up because you'd just lost your parents. How could you still have something to live for? What pushed you forward? And to think that God planned it so perfectly that I went to get water in the back when you called out for help. I would have missed you completely, if it was not for that ring that you wore that night. You said it was from your father, right?"

"Yep. It was the last thing he gave me before he died. I don't think I would have kept going if it wasn't for my parents. They always talked about how proud they were of who I had become, and who I was becoming. I had to go on for them. But I had lost everything that month, my family, my home, and honestly, I was ready to give up my life several times that same month.

"Junior, I have gained so much from meeting you and being your brother. More than what I ever had before, and I know this might seem selfish, but I don't want to lose you, even if it makes you happier when you are with Jessica than me, I can't bear to think of who I will be if you leave."

"Oh, Jeremy. How could you honestly think that Jessica could ever replace you? You are one of a kind. Do you think any of the rest of the family ever thought that they got less time spent with just us when you came into our home?"

"Maybe?"

"No, Jeremy, instead we gained so much more. Think of it this way — your shell collection, if you add one more shell to the rest, do they think that it's worse than before? No, instead, now they are made more complete. A tree with only one branch looks bare and sad until it grows many more, then it looks full, complete, and beautiful. When God adds something to another, He plans it so that His masterpiece becomes more complete.

"Besides, now that I have Jessica, I especially need you as a brother. I mean, me and Jessica might never have officially met, if you hadn't intervened. Yeah, I know what you did; you rascal. When you decided to walk away from the discussion, I wanted to just pull you into the water."

"Haha. I did enjoy that. Your face, when you realized who was behind us, was simply priceless. You really caught the prettiest fish that day."

"Oooh, that's what you had meant. Honestly, I have been wondering about that ever since. Hey, since you have been so helpful with the behind-the-scenes in my relationship with Jessica, would you care to help me, again?"

"Sure, as long as I don't have to do anything stupid."

"Great, because I would like to take Jessica's hand in marriage."

"That's awesome, congrats!"

"Thank you. So, do you think you could help a brother out?"

"I think I could think of something."

Junior and Jessica's wedding day, February 18, 1822, had finally come. Jeremy and Kiley scrambled around, making sure everything was perfect, in order, and on time.

The wedding was held at the church that Jessica practically grew up in, being the pastor's daughter. Junior and Jessica had decided to have an open-door wedding, allowing anyone to come. Later, at the reception, however, only family and the closest of friends were invited.

Since the previous day, Junior was over the top nervous. His body was shaking right up to the point when Jessica came down the aisle. His heart stopped for a split second as he looked upon the beauty of his bride. A smile ran across his face. Jessica was wearing a lovely white dress with small, yellow flowers at the bottom.

At the reception party, Jeremy, Kiley, and Earl made sure that the party lasted well into the night, and even after the bridegroom and bride left, the trio headed out into the garden, bathing themselves in laughter and the moonlight.

"Earl, do you remember when you went outside and took one of mom's pie pans out in the spring mud? You filled it with mud, and then went to Junior and told him that it was Mom's special mud pie."

"Yeah, I can't believe he actually took a bite!"

"Are you serious? What did he think about it?" questioned Jeremy.

"Oh, well, you see, as soon as he took a bite, he just kept it in his mouth until he was sure that Mom wasn't watching, and then he spit it out," replied Kiley.

"We thought he had figured out that it was just mud, but later, when Mom actually served her special chocolate mud pie, he kindly refused it. Kiley and I couldn't hold back our laughter anymore at that point."

"Hahaha. Wow! You guys must have had so much fun!"

"Yeah, but that fun doubled when you arrived. I mean you were like the prank master. We didn't know when you were on our side, or on Junior's," said Earl.

"I did get you good with the snake."

"Ooooh, I remember that. We were going to take a wooden snake covered in some cloth and tie it to Junior's stool so that whenever he moved the stool, it would move with him. It was soooo perfect!" squealed Kiley.

"Yeah, but I guess you were on Junior's side because he said he 'found out about it, from an anonymous source.'"

"Actually, Earl, I never told him."

"What?! If you didn't, then who?"

"Junior told me later that Mom had seen us setting it up, and not liking snakes either, she told him about it."

"Aaaaah," grunted Earl with utter frustration.

"I know what you mean, I was going to get all three of you, but I just had to settle with you two. I actually scared myself as well. When I stuffed that boa skin with pillow stuffing and smoothed it out, I was like, *This thing looks so real!* I remember so well how I had actually forgotten that it was hidden under my bed, behind some boxes. One day, I was taking one of the boxes out and the snake came out, being pulled by a small thread, but it made me jump! I was on my feet and almost ready to run out, when I remembered that I had put it there!

"Dad was just walking by and actually saw it all. He was the one that suggested that I prank someone with it. And then later, you wanted to prank Junior with a snake, and I thought it was the best time to prank you with it.

"The way Kiley screamed when the snake came from underneath the table, and the look on everyone else's face, it was just so priceless!"

"And that was such a long snakeskin. Surely you didn't find all of it in one piece?" questioned Kiley

"No, I actually had to sew some pieces together to make it look almost complete."

"So, Mom was also in on it?" asked Earl.

"No, I did it myself."

"Wow, so you know how to cook, how to sew, how to work the garden, how to wash clothes; you could live all by yourself! At fifteen! That's better than Earl."

"Hey! Fine, it's true. You really are good at everything. Haha."

A moment of silence followed before Earl said, "Well, it seems like Junior knows where he belongs."

"What do you mean, Earl? I thought we all knew where we belonged, here at home. What do you think, Kiley?"

"I'm a little confused as well.

"Well, I know this is home," Earl began, "but I've started to wonder what will happen to me, to us, in the next few years? Or more importantly, what purpose has God planned for me? What am I doing to prepare myself to give up everything and be ready to do anything for our Lord God Almighty? Who am I, in Christ?"

The questions that Earl asked, really got Jeremy thinking. What was God's plan for his life? *Have I been listening to Him? Am I ready for God to call me to anywhere in the world, to do anything? Will I say, 'Here I am, send me,' and then pick up my cross and follow Him?"*

And so, with Junior out of the house, Jeremy fully and earnestly dug into the Word of God. Then one day, as he sat down by the docks, he heard God say something to him... "Go!"

After talking about it with the Lord and Junior, Jeremy told his family what was on his heart, two weeks after God had first told him, "Go!" "I believe that God has called me to be a missionary. But I don't think it is your average kind of missionary. I strongly feel that He wants me to be a missionary on the sea. I know that you are hearing this for the first time now, but

I have been talking about it with Junior, and I have also prayed long and hard about it. I believe that God wants me to go next spring, soon after my sixteenth birthday." Jeremy waited, letting his family take it all in. He didn't know how they would respond, and although he wanted to obey his parents, he knew that if they said, "No," he would have to leave anyway. For how could he not, when the Word of the Lord was so clear to him?

After a long time of sitting and thinking, Jeremy's mother finally stood up and gave him a great big hug. "I love you, son," she said, as the tears began to flow down her face. She realized that her son had reached a point in his spiritual walk that the only right thing to do was to let him go, even though it would mean that he would leave his home, never knowing if they would see him again.

One by one, each member of the Taylor family came and gave Jeremy a hug, a kiss, or a word of encouragement. Each showed their approval and agreement that Jeremy should go, and yet, each realized that their beloved brother would leave them and may never return to them.

After they had all seated themselves once again, Jeremy read from his journal what the Lord had told him each time he prayed, "Jeremy, you have pleased me, and I know now that I can fully trust you in whatever field I lead you to, for you have obeyed my commands. Now, I want you to preach the good news to the poor souls of the sailors at sea. Do not be afraid. I know that you think that you're too young to go on such a journey now, but I will be with you always. I will never leave you, and that's a promise that I gave you many years ago in my Word. You will be kept fed, clothed, and taken care of under my arm—but you must go now. Gather your things for the trip and leave as soon as possible."

So, Jeremy started preparations for a trip across the seas. As he gathered things to take on this new adventure, he also searched in his heart for where God wanted him to go. He began spending many days at the docks, searching for the one and only boat that was to take him across the great ocean. Jeremy wrote down a list of all the things he thought should be a necessity in looking for the correct boat to take him overseas. The boat should be fast and yet quite spacious. It should have living quarters that were up to almost mint condition. His room was to have a great table on which he could write maps and journal his findings. The crew should obviously be of the same belief as he himself was, for then they could encourage him when he needed it. A kind captain would also be ideal. And if God would grant it, he would prefer to travel south and east.

"Junior, I can't wait!" exclaimed Jeremy, as he walked along the docks with his older brother. "I am so excited to see what God has planned for my life. I am going to move mountains, you will see. Demons will fear my name. Pirates will turn from their wicked ways, and they will learn to love the same God I love and follow.

And I am so close to going! I have the money, the food, and all of the supplies to sail off, all I need is a boat and a crew. I haven't had much luck, yet, but I can sense that I will find one soon!"

Junior was silent as his brother talked. He was amazed by how far he had come, and yet, how much farther he had to go. Oh, how far he had to go!

"Junior? What are you thinking about? You are normally much more talkative than this."

"Well...," sighed Junior, "...I'm thinking about you. I'm also excited to see you have this hunger for the Lord, but I must warn you that tough times are ahead and God doesn't always do things the way WE want Him to."

"Brother," Jeremy stopped and looked straight at Junior. "I know. Okay. I know. And I'm going to be ready for that, and I will be flexible and obedient."

Silence filled the air as the two continued to walk down the pier. Then Jeremy saw it. It had everything on his list. This ship in front of him was so perfect. "Junior, this is it. Let's go find the captain and have a tour of the boat." They found him looking at some maps on the front deck. "Good sir, is this your beauty?"

"Yes, it is. Who is asking?"

"Jeremy Taylor. I am looking for someone to take me out to sea. Someone with the exact details of your ship."

"Oh, yes, I have heard of you. Do you have any preference as to where you want to go?"

"Well, I would prefer down south."

"I can arrange that. But it's going to cost you a nifty penny."

"Will this be enough?" Jeremy pulled out a slip of paper containing the amount of money he had saved for the trip. He was prepared.

"I would sure think so."

"Thank you. Thank you. Oh, before I forget, I do have one question. Are you a Christian?"

Aye, I am."

"And your crew?"

"I think almost all of them. Is that a problem?"

"No, I think it will be alright."

"Well then, it's settled. We will be setting sail for South Africa in about two months' time," the captain saw the concern on Jeremy's face. "Something wrong?"

"No, I don't think so. See you then."

Jeremy skipped joyfully home, he felt like a little kid once again. Junior walked slowly behind. *"Two months! That's a long time from now. I thought God had wanted him to go shortly after his sixteenth birthday, which was in two weeks. Father, I know what I must do, but I ask that you give me the strength and the wisdom to approach him in the most loving way. Help him to have an open ear."*

Later that day, Junior and Jessica came for supper at the Taylor house. As they ate, Jeremy told his family what he and Junior had stumbled upon that afternoon. Junior looked toward his father, looking for some hint of agreement, and sure enough, Mr. Taylor locked eyes with his eldest son, concern running across his face.

As soon as dinner was over, Jeremy and Earl bounced upstairs. As the women cleaned the kitchen and dining table, Junior pulled his father aside. "Father, am I the only one that feels that Jeremy is making a mistake?"

"No, son. I feel it, too."

"But it is true that this is definitely the safest way for him to leave the home. But two months! I know what I must do, but how do I do it."

"Well, if you would allow it, I will pray for you."

"Thank you."

"Dear Heavenly Father, we humbly come before you now and ask for your wisdom. I ask that you bestow upon Junior, right now, your infinite wisdom. I understand that Junior doesn't want to ruin any part of the close relationship that he and Jeremy have, so I ask that you guide the two as they go on their own journeys and travels. Amen."

Junior slowly went upstairs. He asked Earl to leave them. He took a deep breath and closed the door to Jeremy's bedroom behind him. Jeremy listened intently, but he could not bear to think that this chance of a lifetime was not God's will.

Junior left a very quiet Jeremy as he went back downstairs, wondering if he should have done what he did. *Was he too hard? What was going to happen to the relationship between him and his little brother?*

Jeremy sat slumped over on his bed. *The boat was just so perfectly ordained by God. Why does Junior not think so? Two months might be a while away, but that would be okay because the boat has literally everything that I ... I ... I. Oh, no! What am I doing?! I know this is your will Father, but please forgive me for taking it into my own hands to ensure its fulfillment, I give it all back."* Jeremy sat all alone, reflecting, thinking, and resoaking into God's promises. Never had he felt so alone and ashamed, but at the same time, he had never known, so well, how great the Love of God was for him.

"Here I am, Lord. Send me. No matter how far and no matter which way you take me, I will follow!" declared Jeremy in his bedroom.

Junior smiled as he heard his little brother shout. He felt overjoyed to know that he was able to be one small stepping-stone placed perfectly by God.

And so, Jeremy went to the docks to tell the captain the news. As he wished them farewell, Jeremy turned around and saw a quaint fishing boat. The crew that came off the ship was surely not of Iceland, but Jeremy felt drawn toward them.

As he approached them, Jeremy wondered, for only a second, what to say before God sent him the aspects that were important to Jeremy's future travels. *"I want you to leave in exactly twenty days."*

"Seriously just that?!... well, okay, if you say so, Father."

Jeremy was able to easily find the captain, as his outstanding leadership was very evident in the room. After having a quick conversation, Jeremy strode out with a big smile.

It was settled, Jeremy was to go with this crew and their boat, *The Messenger."* They were heading back to their homeland, Greenland. And the captain wanted to set sail exactly twenty days from now. Jeremy needed to spend only a quarter of the amount of money that he had saved up. The rest, Jeremy felt led to leave with his family. The total amount that he was able to give to them was around five hundred dollars, which was nothing compared to the value of the amount of love that he was shown by the rest of his family.

The day finally came when Jeremy had to say his goodbyes to his family. Oh! There were tears, both of joy and of sadness. The thought of not seeing each other again dampened many of the people's hearts as they waved goodbye to their friend and brother in Christ—a brother who had flourished in wisdom and experience. He was one of the calmest and most joyful young men in the lovely town.

As Jeremy stepped onto the dock from where the ship and its crew would take him out to sea, he thought of the great memories that he'd built with his family as each one of them said their goodbyes.

"Now, don't you dare get seasick, Jeremy, 'cause if you do, I won't be there to tease you," laughed Earl, as he said goodbye the best way he knew how.

Kiley just fell into her little brother's arms, though he was already six feet tall. She couldn't stop crying, as she knew she would miss him so much that her heart would break. She had really drawn close to him; when she was having a hard time, he would just sit beside her, listen to her troubles, and then give her a great big hug. He was like the big brother that everyone wishes they could have, even though he was the youngest of the family.

After Kiley kissed Jeremy goodbye, his parents gave their son a great big hug and his mom kissed him. Jeremy could see the love that both had for him. They truly were great parents. After a moment of silence, his dad spoke some words of wisdom, as he often did. "Jeremy Taylor, I pray that God will bless you abundantly and that you feel His presence more and more every day. When you doubt and feel like quitting, it might be wise to bring back old memories of your past. Remember how God has always been faithful, always loving, and always caring. He will lead if you will follow. Now, go and ride on the wings of the sea and be free like an eagle."

Lastly, and probably the most heartbreaking for Jeremy, Junior and Jessica came and said their goodbyes. Jessica gave Jeremy a giant hug and a kiss on the cheek, and said, "Now, don't get yourself into too much trouble."

Then Junior gave Jeremy a huge hug, which lasted a really long time, during which some tears were shed. "Jeremy, I don't know what lies before you, the dangers you will face, the fun times, or the souls you will meet. But no matter how far away you go, no matter how alone you feel, and no matter how lost you are, you will always be my little brother. I shall treasure every memory, every bad time and good time, and every moment that we have spent together. I shall treasure it all forever and ever, until the day I die. I will miss you every day of my life, and I will pray for you until we meet again, in this life or the next." Jeremy could only cry and hug his brother. Oh! How painful it was to leave his family, the family that had raised him since he was ten. It had been the best six years of his life, and now he was leaving it all behind. "Could this really be God's plan for my life, at only age sixteen?" he wondered, but then he was reminded of that clear Word of God that he had heard only a month before, "GO!"

And go he did. Jeremy continued to wave goodbye to his family on the dock as the boat left. The family waved back to their son and brother for perhaps the last time.

5

Alone in the Blue Wilderness

As Jeremy waved goodbye to his family from the boat, he was excited about the adventurous voyage that the Lord was taking him on. He thought of the dangers that lay ahead. Even with so many thoughts of the possibilities of being shipwrecked on a deserted island, caught by pirates and taken as a slave, eaten alive by savage cannibals, or even drowning in a storm, he knew that he had the God of the Impossible with him.

Shortly after leaving the dock, the boat headed into some fog. The captain was not quite sure which way to go and was even more turned around when they came out since the sun was blocked by dark clouds. After an hour of looking for a landmark or familiar current that would take them to Greenland, a great storm hit them straight on.

"We're going to die!" many of the crew members yelled, as they tried to keep the ship steady to no avail. As crew members were scattered about, throwing things overboard and bailing water out to keep the boat afloat, Jeremy stayed seated on the deck, as calm as if there were no storm at all. He was praying that if they were really going to die, the Lord would open up the crew members' and captain's hearts. He felt within his heart that these men had not received Christ as Lord, or perhaps they were not right with Him in their life at this moment.

After two hours of trying to keep his boat afloat, the captain finally noticed that his passenger was on his knees and facing starboard. It looked as if his passenger was praying to someone or something, for he also had his head bowed. He had seen some people do the same thing back home. *I will go and see what this man is up to,* decided the captain, since the storm had seemed to pass.

When the captain came near, he asked Jeremy, "What is your name, young man?"

Startled at seeing the captain in front of him, Jeremy was quiet for a few seconds. "My name is Jeremy."

"Well Jeremy, what were you doing?"

"I was praying to my God, who is in Heaven."

"What for?"

"I am asking Him to give you peace."

"Just for me?"

"No. Your crew also."

"Why?"

"Well, first of all, I know it's hard to do anything right when you don't have peace in your heart and your mind. I am also praying that you will have an overwhelming peace, a peace that would fill your entire life because, without peace, our lives are so meaningless, empty, sad, and depressing. They are filled with worry, causing us to always be cautious of what may happen to us, and thereby fearing everything around us."

"You seem very wise. Uh, what did you say your age was?

"Oh, I'm sixteen, sir."

"Hmm, very wise indeed, for such a young one."

By now, many more of the crew members decided to gather around the boy and the captain, to listen in on the conversation.

"This peace that you speak of, is it what helps you to keep calm in a storm like the one we just faced?"

After Jeremy nodded, the captain asked again, "How do I get it?"

Some others that had been listening for a while also chimed in, "I want it, too!"

Jeremy began sharing his testimony of how Jesus saved him, both spiritually and physically, and how he received the greatest peace and its effect on his life. The crew members listened intently as the young man ended his story, ". . . So, as you may very well see when I finally asked the Lord Almighty to come into my heart, free me from all of my troubles, and forgive me of my sins, I could feel that He really did free me and forgive me. I can have peace knowing that He 'knows the plans He has for me, plans to prosper me, and not to harm me, plans to give me a future and a hope.'"

Everyone became very quiet, as they were in deep thought. Then the captain stood up and walked toward where Jeremy stood, in front of the crowd. But he wasn't looking at Jeremy, instead, he had his head bowed. "I have been struggling time and time again with questions in my mind of what my purpose is in life," said the captain with tears in his eyes. "And now I know what it is. My purpose is that I should live for Jeremy's God."

With that, he fell down on his knees and began praying to God. As he prayed, many others came forward and began pouring out their hearts to the Lord. In fact, all of the men came forward and gave their hearts to the Lord. Jeremy, at the age of only sixteen, had brought twenty-three men to Christ in one night.

Shortly after all the men had prayed and had communion together, the storm seemed to have turned around and come straight back to the ship. For the next two hours, these new men were fighting the wind. But now, they were singing parts of hymns led by Jeremy and many wore smiles on their faces, which had, at first, been full of fear. Although they were praying that God would spare their lives, they were all okay knowing they might all go home to Heaven and see Jesus. Jeremy helped the men, as he talked about Jesus and the wonderful things He had done on Earth and how beautiful and lovely Heaven was going to be.

As the minutes ticked by, the boat was beaten this way and that by the waves, and then early in the morning, a huge wave smashed the boat to pieces. Jeremy was knocked unconscious when the wave hit.

When Jeremy finally woke up, he was floating on some driftwood from the destroyed ship. How he came to be on the piece of driftwood, or how he survived the hit from the wave, he didn't know; but He did know that God was in it all.

He floated on the board for many days and nights, drifting along the currents. For the first few days, it seemed as though he didn't go anywhere, as he floated among the wreckage. He gathered many more planks and tied them together with some rope that he had found. He didn't find any food, but he did find some sticks and knives. He found some blankets, and although they were wet, he knew that they could probably dry out. As Jeremy seemed to float away from the wreckage, he had already made a small raft. As he left, he felt sad for the lost crew members, as he didn't find a single living body. But he knew that, in Heaven, there was great rejoicing as the crew came home.

Even though he had no food, he could only think about why God was treating him in this way. Then, after about a week of drifting along the currents, Jeremy realized that God was testing him like Jesus had been tested in the wilderness. He realized that he was alone in a deep blue wilderness.

6

God's Unending Love

As the weeks slipped by, Jeremy became closer to God than he would have ever imagined. The first few days were the hardest for Jeremy. Having no water and no food, he floated on the deep blue currents. As every hour slowly slipped by, he couldn't help but wonder why God had asked him to leave his home. Was it really just so that he could die where no one could see him suffer?

Then, one morning, as he looked out at the endless ocean around him, he thought he saw a ship in the distance. But was it really a ship? Or was it just another hallucination, like others that he'd had—like the giant watermelon the previous day, only it was a giant turtle, not a watermelon? Hallucination or not, Jeremy decided to try to paddle toward it. He soon found out, however, that he was too weak and fainted from exhaustion.

"A'right, lift the young lad up, ladies. Steady now! We don't want the precious cargo to drop back into the sea," yelled the pirate captain.

Once the lad was brought on board and carried into the captain's quarters, the pirate called out once again. "Get back to work, ye scumbags! Biscuit! Go tend to me prize. I want him awake afore dinner."

"Yes, Cap'n!"

It wasn't until midnight that the lad, Jeremy, woke up. He was confused about where he was and how he got there. He got up slowly, taking in his surroundings. He was sitting on a table of some sort, looking out through a wide window. All he saw was the deep blue sea. He was on a ship! But what kind of ship? He looked around, hoping for a clue as to what kind of ship he was on. Behind him, he saw nothing out of the ordinary, but as he looked to his left, he saw some weapons and swords. It was as he turned to the right that he saw a chest. It was shut by several chains and a lock. There was a jar full of keys on a high shelf above it. Also scattered around the chest were bits and pieces of what only a pirate would hold dear. Jeremy walked over to the treasure chest, wondering what great treasures were hidden inside and if it really was a pirate ship that he had landed on.

"I hope you're not trying to steal me treasure, matey."

Startled, Jeremy turned himself around and locked eyes with the pirate. "No, sir. Although I wouldn't mind a peek."

"So, you're a brave fellow. Do you not think that I could slit your throat?"

"True, but I think you would have done it when I came on your ship."

"Maybe I just wanted to hear you squeal like a baby."

"Then, why haven't you done it already?"

The pirate was silent. Never had he seen such bravery in such a young boy. Who was he? And what was it about the boy that really stood out, besides bravery?

Over the next few days, Jeremy and the pirate captain became the best of friends. The two laughed together, worked together, ate together, and even slept in the same room. No pirate in all the seven seas would have thought it possible, a pirate captain and a young castaway. The two were almost inseparable, and yet, Jeremy was still a prisoner on the ship.

The pirate captain, Captain Willy Otterscis, and Jeremy explored every island that they came across in the mid-Atlantic Ocean. On every island on which inhabitants lived, the pirate crew raided their villages and stole all that was of some worth. And after the pirates had finished with their raids, Jeremy would try to calm and minister to the frightened people. At first sight of Jeremy, the men, women, and children became frightened and hostile, for Jeremy looked very much like a pirate, but after listening to his calm, kind voice, they became more relaxed. Many listened intently to the stories that the young boy shared. He was often asked by the men whose hearts were changed when they received a new King into their lives, "If you have such freedom on the pirate ship, and are yet still held captive, why do you not just escape? If you need help, we will happily offer up our services."

But Jeremy would always give the same reason: "The Lord has me right where He wants me to be. For if I ran, wouldn't there be so many more souls that would suffer with pain instead of suffering with joy, if I weren't there to teach them the Way of the Lord, or show them the Joy of the Lord which you also have received? No, I am exactly where I am needed."

Many times, Captain Otterscis watched Jeremy as he entered a village after his crew had raided it. He used to think that Jeremy was going to bolt or maybe rally the villagers for an attack, but it was never so. The only thing the young man ever came back with was a bigger smile than he'd had when he'd entered. But why?

Captain Otterscis decided he would not interfere with the boy's happy business. As long as he never tried to do anything that was unfaithful, he didn't care. Jeremy sailed with the crew for several months. After a year of complete loyalty to the captain, Jeremy ventured to reach members of the pirate crew. Not knowing the result of Otterscis finding out about what he was doing, Jeremy tried to keep it a secret.

However, on one fateful day, Captain Otterscis ordered Jeremy into his treasure room. Jeremy felt like he was walking into the principal's office. As Jeremy stood by the doorway, Otterscis's eyes drilled holes into Jeremy's soul. An awkward silence was heard for the next few minutes. Jeremy shifted nervously. Captain Otterscis had never looked so angry.

Then Otterscis took a deep breath and slowly let it out, "Jeremy. What is this that you are teaching my crew?! Kindness? Love? Caring? Gentleness? WE ARE PIRATES!!!!" yelled Otterscis. "Pirates are pirates! This thing that you have done is unthinkable! Why?! Why?!"

"I was just . . ."

"NO! No, you have said enough! I let you go out to the survivors of our raid... but my own crew mates? No, now you have GONE TOO FAR, Jeremy! This is treason! It is betrayal! But you have been solely loyal to me, and for that, I will send you away peacefully. I want you off my ship! So, take your things, and get on one of those stupid little boats on the side of the ship and sail off to God knows where! Get Out!!"

Rejected by his best friend, Jeremy tried to hold back the tears as he walked past the rest of the crew to his favorite spot on the front tip of the ship. The crew watched a sunken Jeremy go back to his post and gather his things. Many of the men had pity on the young boy. They had grown fond of the boy and hated to see him go out from the ship with not much more than a little food and some water.

Jeremy had only gone a short way off from the boat, when another pirate, Otterscis' second in command, Quaco, called from the crow's nest high over the ship. "Long live Jeremy's God!!!!" And with that, Quaco swung off from the nest and launched into the water. With some help from Jeremy, he hauled himself into the boat. As the two floated out to sea, they looked back at the rest of the crew on the ship. Captain Otterscis was furious and began to bark orders at his men.

The two floated northwards, away on the deep blue wilderness for about a day, before they finally reached land. Through God's guidance and through the winds of change and of the sea, they landed near a port off the west coast of Northern Africa. It was here that Jeremy and his traveling buddy split ways, as they realized that their supplies were running thin. Quaco had also been given a working opportunity, which could have only been the hand of God.

Jeremy had hoped to spend the coming winter on land, but through the Holy Spirit's constant nudge of love, he decided to gather his things and set sail southward to warmer temperatures. By this time, Jeremy was already eighteen, so he decided to buy a small boat and hire a crew with some money that had been given to him through God's grace which had guided a blacksmith to see Jeremy in need, and had unselfishly given him an elegant knife, and a certain sum of money which had been exactly the amount, Jeremy needed, and then some extra.

For several days at sea, Jeremy and his crew fought against the sea in an attempt to travel south, but the winds didn't agree with Jeremy, and they pushed him and his fellow crewmates northward to colder weather. After about a month, the little boat landed once again on the African coast, but after sighting a British flag several times along the way, Jeremy was sure that they were near England.

Winter was right around the corner, but God continued to urge Jeremy to continue his travels. Jeremy refused. Then God came to Jeremy in a dream; it was in this dream that God told Jeremy that he was to go home, and God promised Jeremy that he would reach his destination. And so, Jeremy hesitantly decided that he would do as the Lord bid him to do. But when Jeremy told the rest of the crew, they abandoned him, saying that he was crazy.

Disappointed and rejected, Jeremy sluggishly walked along the docks, as he talked to himself and to God. *"Why does every-thing not work?!"* questioned Jeremy, as he recalled his failures at reaching his pirate captain friend, having to split ways with his traveling pirate friend for lack of supplies, and now being without a crew and left only with a call to go home and a boat that he couldn't sail alone. After an hour of quietness, as Jeremy searched for the Lord's voice, he thought to himself, *"But God has carried me all this way, he must have a great plan for my life. I must trust Him!"*

He spent the rest of the day at the docks. He had a small bag of food and water on his back, as he walked down every dock along the coastline. He kept fighting with what he knew the Lord wanted him to do, and what he felt like doing. Eventually, fear wriggled its way into the brawl, uninvited. *"What if I freeze to death on the way there? Or how about starving to death? Home is a long way from here."*

While walking along the northernmost dock, Jeremy spotted a little boat that was floating just a little way off from shore. It was loose and slowly drifting out to sea.

"Help!!"

Jeremy stopped short. He peered curiously at the little boat.

"Heeellllllp!!!"

Without another moment's thought, Jeremy jumped into the cold water and swam toward the small boat as it floated farther and farther away. Jeremy clambered onto the boat, and as he tried to catch his breath, he looked for the one who had called out. He was shocked. There was no one! "But I know I heard something. I heard something! Or am I really going crazy?! Could it be? No! Maybe. Possibly. God, do you think I've gone crazy?"

"No."

"I didn't think so, but didn't I hear a voice?"

"Yes."

"Well, where is the source?"

"Right here."

"Where? Wait, am I sure I am not going crazy? Because I feel like I am talking to someone, but I haven't seen anybody that has that voice. Where have you been, God?!! Surely you were there when I needed you in that storm three years ago. Couldn't you have saved those men?! Didn't they mean anything to you?! Or what about those people that Captain Otterscis raided; couldn't you have saved their wealth?! Couldn't you have told me to save them?! Couldn't you have reached Otterscis' heart?! Or what about the rest of the crew?! Are they all condemned to burn in Hell?! Could I not have saved more than one?! And why couldn't I have saved the poor soul who called out to me from this boat?!"

"Yours."

"NO! It's . . . it's . . . it's me," sighed Jeremy, realizing that it was his own soul that needed saving. Jeremy sat in the boat a long time before he noticed that he was far off from shore. There were only a few small lights still visible in the night sky. "Well, God, you got me in a boat. Take me home."

7

Home Sweet Home

"Captain, there is a small craft toward the south," shouted the lookout. The captain's ship had been out at sea all day and night. They had been fishing for their island, Surtsey, which was part of their mother country, Iceland.

"What kind of craft is it?" asked the captain.

"I think it's a small sailboat. Wait, I think I can see somebody on there. Shall we go and see if he needs something, Sir?"

"Yes. Maybe he needs some help. Get some blankets in case he is freezing to death out there. Get some food out in case he's starving. By the looks of the boat, he's been out here a very long time."

When they drew nearer, they could see that there was indeed somebody on the small boat, however, he didn't move at all. When they finally reached the boat, they could see that it was a young man, but his body looked white and still. "Men, get something to bring him up. This is an emergency. Johnny, do you have the blankets?"

"Yes, Sir."

"Good. Hey, can you hear me, sir?" The young man had a short scraggly beard like his hair. He was dressed in clothes that looked like a gentleman from Iceland, but he could not tell for sure, as his clothes were ripped up and soiled. In fact, he had no sleeves, and his pants were cut off at his knees. The captain waited for an answer, but none ever came; he realized that the young man was, indeed, unconscious, and probably in need of medical attention as soon as possible.

"Moe, full speed ahead."

Back at the island, the young man was rushed to the nearest hospital. It was soon reported that he surely was not from freezing to death. A month went by, but the young man still didn't wake up, although his heart never missed a beat.

The fishermen decided to go and look for any family that had a missing son on any of the islands. While they were gone, the stranger finally woke up, but the doctors soon found out that he could not remember anything that would be of any use in finding his family. He did not even know his own name, his family, his home village, or how old he was. He even had a hard time speaking without chattering his teeth. Maybe his brain was damaged from being out in the cold for so long.

Another two months went by before they finally discovered his name and where he came from. "Good morning, young man, how are you doing today?" asked the doctor.

"I am doing very well, thank you. In fact, I can speak without chattering now."

"So, you can," realized the doctor, as he listened to the young man's voice. "Can you recall anything from your history, yet?"

"As a matter of a face, yes. As of last night, I can now remember that my name is Jeremy, although I do not remember my last name. I also remember that I was on a missionary trip into the great unknown blue wilderness. My home is in Iceland, somewhere along the coast. That is all that comes to my mind."

"Thank you, Jeremy. The fishermen that saved your life are searching for your family right now. For the time being, you must stay here and rest," ordered the doctor. As he turned away to check on some other patients, he thought to himself, *"This patient may still be a bit crazy–blue wilderness–he was out at sea!"*

For three months, the captain and his crew had been searching for the family without any success. And not having any success on the islands, they had begun a search on the mainland. Eventually, they decided they would try one more village and then return home, get some rest and perhaps some more information, and then return to the search. As they passed through the village, they noticed how, even though Christmas was right around the corner and snow covered the trees, the roofs, and the ground with a thick blanket of fluffy white. It was noticeably quiet as the sun slowly woke up and began to shine its warm rays on the white Earth below. As they passed a small house, they saw a young man with his wife sitting outside, enjoying the sunrise, and a cup of hot cocoa. The couple, seeing the strangers, greeted them and invited them to come inside.

"No, we can't. We have been looking for a family that has lost a son," replied the captain.

"Well, I understand," replied the young man. "Although, you look really tired. Have you any place to sleep?"

"We are quite tired, but we have been searching as quickly as possible, with pretty much no sleep at all. You see, there was a boy we found floating in the middle of the ocean, almost frozen to death. We went to find his parents because when we left, he hadn't woken up for over a month, and the doctors weren't sure if he would make it. So, we have been searching, day and night, but with no luck," replied the captain.

"Well then gentlemen, I say, you must get some sleep soon. Why don't you go over to my parents' house and sleep there? They have plenty of room and will be happy to tell you everything about this town, and maybe even help you find his family."

"Very well then, would you please show us the way?"

"I would be glad to. Would you like to join us, my darling?"

"Yes, please, but let us not forget to wake up the children and take them along."

After a few minutes of walking, the group found themselves at the door of a big house. "Good morning, Junior. What can I do for you today?"

"Well, Father, these men are fishermen, from the island of Surtsey, in search of a family that may have had a missing son. They need a place to rest before continuing on their journey."

"We will be happy to have them rest here. What did you say your name was?"

"I am Captain Charlie and this is my crew."

"Well, if you aren't too tired, I am sure my wife would enjoy making breakfast for you. We have pancakes and homemade pancake syrup. Junior and Jessica, will you join us too? We would enjoy your company. I feel in my spirit that we need to pray for Jeremy, again. Shall we have a prayer meeting sometime in the afternoon? I will invite your brother and sister and their families as well."

"Thank you, Father. I think we will stay; after all, it's almost Christmas."

After breakfast was over, the fishermen made their way upstairs to their own bedrooms. Time went by, and as the fishermen slept on till lunch, the other families arrived and started preparing lunch.

"Hey Dad, Mom says it's time to wake up our guests so we can all eat!" called Kiley.

Mr. Taylor got up from the couch and went upstairs to wake up their guests. When they all came down, they sat around the table and Mr. Taylor started off with prayer. "Our Heavenly Father, you know all things and you see all things. Father God, we thank you for the many blessings you have given us. Father, we pray a special prayer of protection on our son, Jeremy, whom you sent into the great unknown as a missionary, about three years ago. We thank you for this wonderful day you have given us and that you sent your Son to Earth. Bless this food to our bodies and help these fishermen find the family who has lost their son. Amen. Alright, let's eat."

As they ate, Lily, the daughter of Junior and Jessica Taylor, noticed that Johnny, one of the crew, was thinking hard about something. "Mista Johnny, what you thinkin' about?"

"Oh, little one, I was thinking of that picture that is hanging on the wall. It looks very familiar. What do you think, Captain?"

"Let me see. Yes, it does look familiar. Funny though, I don't have the strangest clue why."

"The picture is of our adopted son, Jeremy. He felt a calling from the Lord to be a missionary at the age of fifteen. We have not seen him since the day he left, but we have peace from God that we will see him again. Although, we do not know if it will be in Heaven or on Earth," said Mrs. Taylor.

"Captain, may I have a word alone with you?" asked Johnny.

"Yes. Will you excuse us?"

As they left the room, the captain asked, "What is it, Johnny?"

"Well, if I am not mistaken, I feel that the boy we rescued is their son."

"I have the same feeling. I think it is the Lord that has brought us together. Yes, I have decided to take them along to see their son."

The two entered again and when lunch was over, the captain asked, "Taylor family, do you have any specific plans for the coming weekend?"

"Hmmm… I don't think we have any specific plans. Why do you ask?" replied Mr. Taylor.

"Well, you see, I believe…" the captain took a small pause before continuing, "… we believe that the boy we found on the ocean is your boy, Jeremy."

"Are you sure, Captain?" asked Junior.

"Yes, I am pretty sure. That picture looks very much like him, only he has a beard. But yes, I am sure that the two are the same man." Then, all of a sudden, his face changed from happiness to sadness. "We must take you to him. When we left him to go find his family, he was still fighting for his life. He was hanging on by a thread."

The family wasn't sure what to feel. Excitement at the possibility of seeing their beloved son and brother or worry for his health and safety? One thing was sure, they must go and see him before it was too late. So, the entire family boarded a ship, along with the captain and his crew, to set sail to Surtsey.

As the ship passed by a beach, the Taylor family noticed the remains of a ship that had landed on the rocks. Lily asked, "What happened over there?"

"Oh, you mean on the beach?" After Lily nodded, Charlie continued, "You see, three years ago, there was a great storm at sea. There was a ship that had left port and had been out at sea for only a few hours when it got caught in the storm. The ship didn't make it, and we found no survivors. These are the remains of the ship that came ashore."

"Do you know the name of the ship?" asked Kiley, who sounded a bit worried.

"Yes, it was the Messenger."

"What?! That was the same ship that Jeremy was on!" exclaimed Kiley. "How on Earth did Jeremy survive that?!"

"Here we are!" announced Charlie.

"Wow, this is so beautiful!"

"It's gorgeous!"

"Wonderful!"

"Well, thank you."

Just then, a young boy came running toward the captain. "I heard you were coming home, and so I have been sent to tell you that the boy you rescued has awakened from his slumber. He is doing much better now."

"Thank you, boy. Now, we can either all go and see Jeremy, though I do think it would perhaps be too overwhelming for him, or I could take you to my home and then take some of you to him. Although, I don't know if he will be awake or...."

"I think it might be best to go to your home," interrupted Mr. Taylor, "and decide there, who will go with you to see Jeremy. Can we all agree with that?"

"Yes," everyone replied back.

Once they reached the home of Captain Charlie and his wife, Darla, the Taylors quickly decided that it would be best if the kids all stayed there, along with Earl and Darlene, Robert and Kiley, and Jessica, so that Junior and his parents could go with Charlie to see Jeremy at the hospital.

Later, at the hospital, Charlie was surprised to see that the boy had recovered almost completely, except that he couldn't remember everything. "Hello, sonny. Could you tell me your name?"

"My name is Jeremy."

"Well, Jeremy, I have some people that would like to see you, would you like to see them? They're your family."

"Yes, please."

Charlie brought Jeremy's family into the room.

Jeremy's mom was in shock and in tears. *Could this really be her son?! After all these years, her son had finally come home!*

Mr. Taylor and Junior both stood stock-still, as they began to take it all in. Their son, their brother, was home.

Jeremy stood frozen. Not breathing. The doctor was worried for a moment that he didn't remember until he saw a tear run down the young man's cheek. Jeremy was starting to remember. As each memory flooded his brain once more, tears streamed down his face. Junior hesitantly came closer, not knowing if his brother recognized him or not, and Jeremy fell into his brother's arms, sobbing for joy. He had found his family. He had come home.

Mr. and Mrs. Taylor went back with Charlie to his house, while Junior stayed with Jeremy until he was free to go.

When Charlie and the other two Taylors reached the house and opened the door, they found the rest of the family all waiting in anxious anticipation of what news they had.

"It's him," said Mrs. Taylor, as she began to cry once more. Kiley ran into her mother's arms as both cried tears of joy. Earl came and gave his dad a big hug.

After some more tears were shed, the family went into the living room. Earl was the first to ask, "So, how is he doing?"

"Well, surprisingly, he's holding up alright. Although we didn't ask him too much about his time out at sea. It's amazing to think that he survived on a little boat since the Messenger shipwreck."

"That's absurd. That means he would have had to have survived for three years on that little boat."

"Yeah, well, with our God, nothing is impossible!"

After a period of silence, Jessica asked, "Where's my husband?"

"Oh, yes, thank you for reminding us, Jessica," replied Mrs. Taylor, "He stayed with Jeremy, and we were going to tell you when we reached here, but I guess it's still overwhelming that Jeremy is alive and now home."

"If you wish, the captain would be happy to take you to Junior. Don't worry about the kids, we'll take care of them."

"Oh, thank you. I would really like to go. When can we go, Captain?"

"Whenever you are ready."

Soon, Jessica walked out the door and went to the hospital with Charlie.

When they reached the hospital, Charlie pointed out to Jessica which room to enter and then returned home.

Jessica found Junior beside Jeremy as he slept. Jessica could easily see that Junior had been crying, and at first, she thought it was just happiness to see that Jeremy was here; but knowing her husband, she realized it was something more than just that. "What's wrong, honey?"

"Well, Jeremy was telling me about what happened that first day when he left the harbor. He was hardly able to stay awake for the entire story. In fact, he actually fell asleep before he told me how he survived the shipwreck. His whole body is exhausted. I don't know what he's been through, but as exhausted as he is, it seems like he's been through hell. The doctor said that this is the best he's slept since he arrived here. He was saying that, at first, Jeremy kept having nightmares multiple times every night. But now, he's been smiling in his sleep the whole time. He knows he's home and with family. What a great feeling that must be!"

Over the next several weeks, the Taylor family decided to take shifts to watch over Jeremy. Charlie had readily opened his doors to the Taylor family while they stayed in Surtsey, and with much convincing, the family conceded. Junior and his family stayed for the first week, then Robert and Kiley, Earl and Darlene, and then Mr. and Mrs. Taylor. The families quickly learned that Jeremy tended to sleep through the day, sometimes several days in a row. He woke up for only a few hours at a time, often at night. Even though Jeremy tended to wake up at night, he was overjoyed to see his family in the hospital room. His nightmares were finally over. He was home.

Finally, the day came when Jeremy was released from the hospital. His whole family came to see him as he came out of the hospital with Junior and Jessica. Jeremy smiled when he saw his entire family waiting for him. How much they had all grown, and so many new loving faces he was able to call family.

There were Junior and Jessica and their kids, Lily, Brittney, and Triss, the latter two being identical twins. Then, there was Earl and his wife Darlene. They had their young boy, Jimmy. And then there were Robert and Kiley, who had only been married for about six months.

The day that Jeremy was released from the hospital was a day filled with laughter and joy. When the rest of Charlie's crew heard that the young boy was released from the hospital, they decided to go see the young man a few days later. On one particular evening, Jeremy decided to tell his story of being out in the deep blue wilderness.

The families that wanted to hear the young man's story gathered together in a nearby church building. The people that came to see Jeremy and hear his story were those that were on Charlie's crew the night they discovered the frozen young man on the little boat, their families, and some of the hospital staff and their families.

Jeremy welcomed each one inside, along with his brother, Junior, and Captain Charlie. One person Jeremy recognized immediately was Johnny, one of the crew members with Charlie. He had someone with him, whom he introduced, "This is Victoria. She's my cousin. Her dad died in a storm at sea. He was on the same ship as the one you were on when you left Iceland, Jeremy."

"I'm very sorry for your loss, my lady," Jeremy said.

"It's okay. Although, I never knew that there was a survivor from the ship. I thought everyone had died. Are you sure you were on the same ship? Pardon me for the curiosity, it's just hard to believe."

"I understand. Maybe you could describe your father, I may remember him."

"Well, he was the captain of the ship, very open to what others had to say, a good listener and leader. He was a man of high respect among his crew. He was never afraid of a storm, never afraid to die, except for the fact that it would leave me all alone. My mother died when I was very young, and I had no siblings. He had some gray hair and always wore a captain's hat. The hat had a small feather sticking out at the top of it. The result of a five-year-old."

"In that case, yes, your father was a fine captain. I am proud to let you know that your father died a very happy man. He received Jesus as his Savior before the last wave crashed into the ship." Seeing the wonder and curiosity on Victoria's face, Jeremy asked, "Are you a Christian?"

"To be honest, no. But I have heard many stories of the great legend."

"Well, I assure you that after tonight, you will know that He is not just a legend. Come on, the story is about to start. I'm just going to get a jug of water, so my throat doesn't dry up completely. See you around."

"Yeah, see you."

The next few hours were spent by Jeremy talking about all that had happened to him over the past few years. He spoke of all the hardships, trials, and good times that he had gone through. He had gone through several shipwrecks, many of which he'd barely survived. He faced many pirates and landed on many beautiful islands. He had met natives, sailors, pirates, and other stranded people that were shipwrecked. Many of the people he had met ended up being saved or at least sparing his life. God blessed him time and time again, as he remained faithful throughout the tough times.

"I don't remember exactly how I ended up in the boat, or how I was able to sail near home; I sometimes think I remember catching glimpses of someone towing the boat, but it is not clear.

"I truly believe that I would never have survived everything that I've been through if it weren't for the constant and consistent love of God. When I felt like giving up, God would lavish upon me His love, His grace, and His mercy. There was never a moment that I didn't have to trust in God. It sure was a tough three years. But I have come to live by the verse Jeremiah 29:11 which says, 'For I know the plans I have for you,' declares the Lord. 'Plans to prosper you, and not to harm you. Plans to give you a hope and a future.' And also, Romans 8:28, 'And we know that in all things God works for the good of those who love him, who have been called according to his purpose.'"

There was silence, as each was in awe of what this young man had gone through. Earl's chin dropped to the floor as he looked over at his wife's paper; she had been writing throughout Jeremy's storytelling. After asking for permission to read it out loud, Earl spoke up, "I have a paper here. Well, actually, it's my wife's paper. Anyway, a paper that contains all of the different times something tough came to you, Jeremy. My wonderful and beautiful wife wrote them down as you told us your story."

"Well, let's hear it."

"So, you experienced two shipwrecks, landed on three is-lands that you know were inhabited by cannibals, and met five pirate ships, four of which you battled with alongside Captain Otterscis. You met four other sailing ships, went through eleven storms, were thrown overboard by pirates two times, and were robbed three times. Not to mention the number of times you didn't have any food or water, or a safe place to stay, and the countless other things that you must have faced, that you don't quite remember."

Silence once again filled the room, even Jeremy, who had gone through it all, was surprised at how much he had gone through. *How did I survive all that?* he wondered.

"No wonder you were so tired, little brother," said Earl.

"And I would do it all again if it meant that many would hear and receive the Good News of Jesus. But maybe after a month-long nap and Mom's homemade cooking. Haha."

After a brief moment of silence, Jeremy summarized, "How great, powerful, and amazing is the God we live to serve!"

8

Rest in God

The following days were wonderful for the Taylor family. The family explored all the beautiful sites and met several wonderful people. Jeremy visited every one of the crew members who were on the ship that saved him only a few months prior, including Johnny, with whom Victoria lived.

"Well, good afternoon, Jeremy. Welcome! Supper will be ready in a bit. Victoria is a really good cook. Please come and sit down over here. Victoria, would you like to share our news now or later?"

"Oh, I think I would like to do it now. I'll be there in a minute."

As soon as Victoria was standing nearby Johnny, she started, "Well, we are happy to announce to you that we have both received Jesus Christ as our Lord and Savior, and it's all thanks to you! Your story was amazing, and we knew that we both wanted to have the same joy and peace that you have."

"That is awesome! I am really proud of you. May the Lord bless you as you grow in Him."

After talking a little more, Victoria was called back to the kitchen by the oven timer, as the chicken was just finished baking. Soon after, Jeremy found out how good Victoria's cooking actually was—it was DELICIOUS!!! After supper, Johnny had an errand to run and wasn't going to be back for a while, so he left Jeremy and Victoria to talk.

Jeremy found out that Victoria's mom had passed away when she was only seven, and her dad had passed away three years ago on the same ship that Jeremy first set out on. Her mom had drowned in an icy cold lake when she was caught in a storm while riding a horse. She couldn't see where she was headed and rode straight off a cliff's edge and into the lake.

Victoria had been in school until the year that her dad died when it became too hard for her to complete high school after losing her dad. It was a time that was mentally, physically, and emotionally hard for her. She had fallen into a deep depression and was only able to get back on her feet with the help of her cousin, Johnny.

"Jeremy, why would God take my parents away? Why would He allow me to go through all of that if He truly is a merciful and loving God? Why? Why?" cried Victoria.

After a moment of silence, and comforting Victoria, Jeremy replied, "Listen, I don't know why He does the things He does, but that's where faith comes in. I choose to believe that God has plans for me that are for my good, even when it all seems to be going bad. I lost my parents when I was about ten. Both of them died the same day and from the same illness. I've asked God why he couldn't have saved them, but then I wonder if I would have ever known the Lord as I do now. I might never have become a missionary, so I wouldn't have had this testimony to share, and you may never have received Christ as your Savior. We can never truly understand why God does the things He does or allows bad things to happen to good people. Instead, we must have faith that His plan and His love are greater than ours."

The time sped by as the two talked, cried, and comforted each other. As Jeremy left the house, he knew, as did Victoria, that their lives would never be the same and that they would meet again.

On the morning of Captain Charlie's birthday, the Taylor family departed from port to get home. But a storm rolled in just as their ship passed the Captain's lighthouse, and not wanting to relive Jeremy's traumatic experiences, they decided to return to port. So, they decided to crash the birthday party.

At the birthday party, the crew was having a blast when there was a knock on the door. "I'll get it, Charlie. Just keep those boys from the kitchen," said Darla. She opened the door, and the people that stood there surprised her. "I thought you would be on your way home by now!"

"Well, we aren't going to do that in this weather. Mind if we join the party?" asked Jeremy.

"Oh, yes. We are actually celebrating Charlie's birthday. Hey Charlie! You've got some old friends here."

"Well, I wouldn't call us old, but I wouldn't be surprised if this old man was getting, well, old," teased Mr. Taylor.

"Only if old means 'One Little Dude' then yes, I am old because I am ageless in spirit, mind, and soul," the captain fired back, as he spun around to see the culprit of such an insult. "Ah, my old friends are back! Hey, boys, it's the Taylor family, again. Get out of the kitchen and welcome our long-lost friends, hahaha!"

"I wouldn't consider us lost or long. Are you sure your clock is working, 'old' friend?" retorted Mr. Taylor.

"My clock?! No, my clock is working better than yours. Now, why don't you calm down, and tell me how you've come to be so cold—and by cold, I mean 'Clueless, Old, Lost, and Dull'—because your words are duller than a butter knife."

As the two continued to roast each other, Jeremy noticed Victoria in the kitchen and slowly went over. Johnny smiled slightly, as he watched Jeremy walk over, and then turned back to the hostile fight that was going on.

"Well, good evening, miss. You are looking splendid tonight."

"Thank you, young sir. And you're looking, well, cold and wet."

"Why, I've just been out at sea!"

"Then, let's get you a towel." With that, Victoria quickly went to fetch Jeremy a towel, and then they went out onto the porch outside to watch the storm.

Back inside, the victor of the battle was about to be decided, "I think your senses are all dying, sir," retorted Charlie, "'cause you can't see that I'm a pirate, and me crew is robbin' everything right from under yur nose. You can hardly hear me anymore, and ya can't feel yur legs from standin' so long! You can't smell the food that's a cookin' in the kitchen, and I'm sure, as Heaven is real, that when ya eat some of the food, ya won't even be able ta taste it."

"Well,… uh. You… uh. No, I got nothing. You win, Captain. Now, what do you mean by you're stealing everything from under my nose?"

"Why, we've stolen some of your kin!"

"Who?"

"Jeremy."

"Wait, where is Jeremy?"

"Oh, you mean the love birds?"

"What?!"

"Yeah, the two are over there on the porch, sir. We've stolen Jeremy right from under your nose," said Johnny.

Then Mr. and Mrs. Taylor, along with their kids, all looked toward the porch behind the crew, and sure enough, saw the two holding hands and staring out at the beautiful skies that were now slowly beginning to clear as the storm began to recede.

"Seems like you'll be staying here a while longer," said Charlie.

The rest of the evening rushed away. The food was amazing, and Mr. Taylor burned his tongue on the first bite, making it hard for him to taste the rest of the food for a short while. Everyone had a blast. As they sat around in the living room, there was so much noise as the kids played, and the men talked, joked, and teased. Junior, however, noticed that Jeremy was abnormally quiet that night, but he was sure that it was because of Victoria.

For Jeremy and Victoria, time seemed to speed by all too quickly, as their relationship bloomed and prospered. Jeremy's family had sailed back home shortly after the Captain's party, while Jeremy stayed on the aisle with his girlfriend.

Jeremy spent his time on the island working with several missions and resting in God's peace. He enjoyed spending his time with the people that were in need, but he enjoyed his time most when he was able to share it with Victoria, the pearl of his dreams.

About two years later, now the age of twenty-one, Jeremy asked Junior to come back to the isle along with his family, to help him with some things. In the days that followed, Jeremy had some private meetings with Junior and then began spending most of his time in shops and out on the docks. He also spent a little bit of time here and there in Charlie's lighthouse. Jessica spent time with Victoria whenever Jeremy said that he had some "business" to attend to at the docks. And when Victoria asked Jessica what they were doing here, she simply replied that Junior and Jeremy were "helping the sailors at the docks, fixing up the lighthouse, and running errands."

"Oh," was the short, curious, and confused reply.

A few days went by, and eventually, Junior and Jeremy stopped going to the docks as often and began spending more time with family. Then, one fine afternoon, Jeremy took Victoria to the docks. The port and the lighthouse were situated on the southern tip of the isle and were so positioned that it was possible to watch the sunset on one side of the port and then take a short walk around the tip to watch the moon climb up the starry skies.

As they watched an incredibly gorgeous sunset, they also enjoyed some of the isle's most loved delicacies. Once finished eating, Victoria asked, "So, how was my handsome love able to afford such expensive and delicious food?"

"Well, let's just say that God provides the needs and desires of those that seek Him."

"Well, you are amazing. So, what have you planned for the rest of the evening, my rusty sailor?"

"Well, I've been studying the stars, just as any 'old rusty sailor' would, and I've been talking with some experts enough to know that there will be a fine and beautiful moon out tonight. Shall we go around the tip and see it for ourselves?"

"Yes, we shall."

As they neared the tip, Jeremy told Victoria to close her eyes and hold his hand. He then led her onto a dock that barely had any ships tied to it and told her to open her eyes.

As she did, her jaw dropped, "Jeremy, that is the most beautiful full moon I've ever seen! It's so perfect, and the stars, oh my... what a beautiful night! But that moon... it's just so, so, so, perfect. It's like a, like a...,"

"Like a pearl," finished Jeremy.

"Exactly! Like a pearl." She began to swirl around to hug her love, "It's so beauti–"

Jeremy was down on one knee, "Victoria, you are the pearl of my life. Not a day goes by that I don't think about you, and I know that you are the most beautiful pearl in the whole world, more beautiful than any moon, star, or jewel. Victoria Esther Flowers, will you marry me?"

Through all the tears, she was able to nod and say, "Yes!"

At that moment, a boat's horn blew on the distant waters. After this horn blew, several others also blew. Soon, almost every boat around the dock was blowing their horns, as Jeremy swung his love around. After all the sound of the horns faded away, candles were lit—hundreds of candles. It was like the entire dock was lit on fire.

But the surprises didn't stop there. The distant boat that had blown its horn first was coming into port. As soon as it was tied down, there was much cheering, and then from the boat, off stepped Johnny, and behind him, the rest of the Taylor family. Victoria was at a loss for words. There was so much excitement. That evening seemed to fly by way too fast, and before long, it was midnight.

About six months later the couple got married—and their wedding was awe-dropping. They hosted the wedding ceremony near the lighthouse, and after the reception and party, the couple fled the scene on a boat that Jeremy was able to borrow for a while.

For the next few years, Jeremy rested from the hard past that he had gone through. He knew that God was giving him time to spend with his growing family. So, that is exactly what he did. He took all the time he could to rest and relax, for God was not finished with him yet.

9

A Little Faith

Five years had passed, and time had found Jeremy and Victoria settled a few miles further inland from Jeremy's parent's house. Jeremy and Victoria had two children, Christopher and David—David was the eldest at three-and-a-half, and Christopher was two. Although Jeremy loved to spend time with his family and friends, he missed being on the mission field he'd left four years before. When he told Victoria about his desire to be a missionary again, she told him that she too wanted to go out into the world to share the Good News with the sailors, pirates, and natives or cannibals. So, the couple began praying that they would be able to serve outside of Iceland, once again, in their Father's vast Kingdom.

In the spring of 1836, three years later, Jeremy and Victoria finally heard the answer to prayer.

"One, two, three, four, five . . .," Christopher counted his toys. His parents had told him and his older brother, David, that they planned to go away on a trip for God and asked if they wanted to stay here with their grandparents or come along with them. They both answered, each in their own cute little way, "Yes!"

"So, which is it? Grandparents or us."

"Yes!"

"Which is it?"

"Sailors!"

It was then that Jeremy also decided that they would plan to leave two months later. There was a week left to buy a boat that was for sale, and they still had about a thousand dollars left.

It was devotional time, and as Christopher listened intently, a verse stuck with him. ". . . go, sell all your possessions and give to the poor, and you will have treasure in Heaven. Then come and follow me."

"Well," thought Christopher, *"I have a lot of toys that I could sell. And besides, I have treasure in Heaven and want to follow Jesus. As for giving it to the poor, I'll give it to my parents. I mean, don't poor people kind of not have any money? My parents seem to not have any money right now because they can't seem to pay for the boat. Then, it's settled."*

So, in the morning, he gathered all of his toys and told his parents that he was going outside for a while. He found a big box and carried it to a spot on the corner where he knew a lot of people passed by. He displayed all of his toys and began his little business. When a customer asked him how much for a toy, his response was, "Whatever Jesus leads you to give, it doesn't matter, give to Jesus."

All that day, Christopher sold his little toys. He came home every now and then to get a drink or eat a snack, and then went outside again to continue selling his toys but didn't tell anyone what he was doing. Everybody that passed by and heard his response was surprised, especially when they found out that he was only five. Finally, he'd sold all his toys and came home about an hour before supper, but he still didn't tell anyone. Instead, he put the money into an envelope and put it into the mailbox.

That night, in their bedroom, Jeremy and his wife were looking through their mail. "Wow, what a miracle. Look at this!" exclaimed Jeremy to his wife.

"What is it?" she asked.

"This envelope was in the mail when I came home today but has no address or anything," Jeremy said, holding it out so that she could see it. "It contains exactly $1,000. Praise be to God the Most High and the God of the Impossible!"

"Yes, let us thank Him now. Oh, I wish I could know who gave us this amazing gift."

The next day, as the family sat around the table, Jeremy read from the newspaper, "Well, listen to this Victoria, 'A little boy spends the day on a street corner selling his toys.' Do you know who it could be?"

"Why, that looks like Christopher! Christopher, was that you?"

"Maybe."

"Now, why on earth would you do that?!"

"Well, Jesus said that I should sell all that I have and give it to the poor. And doesn't poor have to do with no money? And you don't sound like you have any money, so I gave it to you."

"Well, thank you so much, but what about all of your toys, won't you miss them?"

"Yes, but I will have treasure in Heaven, and now I will follow Jesus, like you."

"How did you manage to get all of this money? Did you overprice your toys? You know that's not right."

"No, I told customers to pay whatever Jesus told them to pay—and that's what they did."

"Alright then, let us go buy the ship, pack up, and follow Jesus!"

A few weeks later, after saying goodbye to their families, Jeremy and his family sailed out on their own ship, with God leading them through the winds, not knowing if they would ever come back again.

10

At Sea, Trusting God

The sun had just gone down on the Northern Atlantic Ocean. Jeremy and his family had been at sea for about six months. They had enjoyed the adventures, beautiful scenery, and the opportunity to share the Gospel.

The family had no idea where they were, but they weren't worried about it. Why should they be worried? Their God was in control, and He was carrying them wherever He wanted them to be.

"Well, Father, it looks like there is a ship in the distance. What do you make of it?'

"I would have to agree, son. It also looks like there is a big storm heading our way. I think we need to get the troops together and see what the Commander says, Little David."

"Right away, Daddy."

The family met in the small cabin room that they had learned to call home. Once they were all in the room, Jeremy began,

"Everyone, there is a ship coming toward us. It looks like a ship from England. I know that they are probably friends, but we still must ask God for guidance. Let us bow our heads and find out if we should attempt to meet them or not."

So that is exactly what the Tayler family did. All four of them got down on their knees and began to pray and wait patiently for an answer. "Our Heavenly Father, we come to you in peace and a desire to do your will with all of our hearts, minds, and souls. Father, we want to thank you for all of the things that you have provided for us, such as a fine ship, a wonderful family, food every day, and the ability to share the Good News to all that pass by. God, we also thank you for sending your Son to Earth to die for us and other sinners alike. And now Father God, we ask that you bless us and give us another chance to share your Word. As you know, there is a ship coming our way, so we would like to know if we are to attempt to contact them or if we should just pass by. Your Kingdom come, Your Will be done, On Earth as it is in Heaven. Amen."

After prayer, the family sat waiting and waiting. It didn't matter anymore how long it would take to receive an answer, for they knew that whatever happened, it would be God's will.

Time slipped by as the family sat waiting, and although the family was sure that the ship had passed by already, they stayed. For who could tell what God's plan was? The family had learned that even if they were sure of something, they should not leave God's presence unless they were told to; they should not take matters into their own hands. Even if the outcome would be the same. It didn't matter.

—————

Booooom! The family was startled. They had fallen asleep and now had awakened with the sound of thunder. David felt compelled to go look outside. "Father, come look at this."

"What is it, son?"

"It's a huge dark cloud just behind us."

As the family gathered around to see the dark clouds, little Christopher spoke up, "Thank you, Jesus, for letting us sleep through the big storm."

"Shall we thank Him for His Promises?" suggested David.

"Yes. Let's bow our heads. David, do you want to pray?"

"Sure. Father God, we thank you for giving us an answer. Thank you for taking us through another storm once again. Thank you for a sturdy ship. We also thank you for giving us strength and guidance to get through every hardship." As he was about to close with an "Amen", he slightly opened his eyes and then quickly added, "And thank you for land. Amen."

Immediately, everyone opened their eyes to see if what David had said was true. Sure enough, there was land not far off. "Hurrah!" cried little Christopher, "I thought we would never again see land."

"Couldn't have said it better myself, son. Say, why don't we stay there, wherever that might be, for a while."

"Fine by me, Dad," replied David.

"Yep, I think I like land a little more than water if that's okay," said Christopher.

"Yes, that is fine. We all have different things we like and different callings from God. It might just be that God will call you to a life on land, but it won't matter, as long as each of us follows the unique and special calling that God has given to us."

"Thank you, Mommy. I'll try to remember that."

"Ahoy, sea lovers. Welcome to Norway! How are you doing on this fine day?" called out a rustic bearded man, whose roundness was showing from beneath his torn coat.

"Ahoy!" replied Jeremy, as he helped secure the ship to the dock. "We are all doing fine. Tell me, kind sir, what day is it? And who do we have the pleasure of meeting?"

"My friends call me Captain Cat, for I always carry a cat wherever I go, his name is Seven Sail. My real name is Humphry Johnson, but you can just call me Captain Cat if you like. Oh, and the day is... well, to be honest, I can't remember, and I normally don't care. But I have a calendar inside my house."

"Thank you very much. My name is Jeremy Taylor, and this is my wife, Victoria Taylor. These are our boys, David and Christopher."

"Why don't you come over to my house, my lighthouse to be exact, and stay for the night?"

"I think we would enjoy that very much. What do you say, kids, shall we go for a tour of a lighthouse?"

"Hurrah!!!!" chirped David and Christopher. Then David asked. "What's a lighthouse?"

"Ooh, I know, I know," said Christopher. "It's a light big enough to be a house, right?"

"Not exactly, little one. Come on! Follow me, and I'll show you," replied Captain Cat. "And just so you know, it's quite a long walk from here. I come here, though, because this is one of my favorite fishing places."

11

Joy Forevermore

After the kids were sent to bed in the lighthouse, Jeremy and Victoria sat down with Captain Cat, and Seven Sail curled up against his neck. The two shared everything that they had gone through.

". . . and now God has brought us here to Norway. There is so much to thank Him for."

Jeremy and Victoria had been looking down for most of the sharing, but now, as they both looked up, they saw that the captain had tears running down his face.

"Captain Cat, have you ever received Jesus Christ as your personal Savior?" Victoria quietly asked.

"Yes, I did, but that was when I was about thirteen. I fell away from Him only a few months after I received Him into my heart. I have rededicated my life to Him several times, but every time trials came, I would turn bitter and hard. So, I don't understand how you could have so much joy through every hardship that you have gone through. It just doesn't make sense. How can you be joyful when you've seen loved ones die all around you? I don't know how that joy is possible." Tears continued to stream down the captain's face.

"It might be hard for you to understand, but you see, we receive this joy directly from the Lord Jesus Christ. He is the One, the only One, that can give us the joy we have when we face hardship. But you have to know that every time we face hardship, it's not easy to stay joyful. Most of the time, we feel like just giving up and being pessimistic about the whole situation. However, whenever those thoughts came to our minds, God sent a Bible verse to our ears—Jeremiah 29:11 says, 'For I know the plans, I have for you,' declares the LORD, 'plans to prosper you, and not to harm you, plans to give you a hope and a future.'"

"Can you pray for me?" asked Captain Cat.

"Yes, we can. But you need to ask and seek out the relationship with God for yourself. It is only through a close relationship with our Father that we can stay joyful."

"Alright, I will."

As the Captain began to pray silently in his heart, the Taylors prayed for their new-found friend. "Our Heavenly Father God, you are the Most High, the Almighty, the One and Only God, and you are our Savior. Father, we come before you today in obedience to your will. Our friend is calling out to you today, for he yearns to know you more. He desires to have your everlasting joy. Father God, we ask that you meet him now, in this place. Bless him with an overabundant joy—a joy that never ends, even though trials may come his way. I ask that you give your son a feeling of joy right now—a feeling that he will never forget.

In your name, Jesus, we declare right now that your peace and your joy fill this place. Amen."

Immediately after the prayer, they heard a scream from upstairs, and Victoria ran to see what was wrong. As Captain Cat got up from his knees, Jeremy could see that this was a new man, for he no longer carried the sorrow that he had carried on his back for so many years; but he was now filled with joy—a joy that would never stop, and never die because his joy came from Jesus, who was, and is, and will forever be eternal.

Victoria came down with a smile on her face as she said, "When I got upstairs to the children's rooms, I saw something unusual. They were both wide awake. Christopher was singing happy songs, and David was dancing to the songs. When I asked them why they were so happy, they told me that they were just so full of joy, they simply could not sleep. But I told them they had to, or they wouldn't be able to go to the top of the lighthouse tomorrow. They literally bounced into bed. Hahaha."

"Wow! It's amazing how God moves!" exclaimed Captain Cat. "Thank you for praying for me. I feel so complete and fulfilled."

"Well, that's how we feel when a hardship or trial comes our way. We just face it with Jesus and with joy. James 1:2-3 says, 'My brethren, count it all joy when ye face trials of all kinds, knowing this, that the trying of your faith worketh patience.' And Philippians 4:6-7 says, 'Do not be anxious about anything, but in every situation, by prayer and petition, with thanksgiving, present your requests to God. And the peace of God, which transcends all understanding, will guard your hearts and your minds in Jesus Christ.'"

"Well, I can't thank you enough for helping me. I feel like I truly am a changed man."

"Don't thank us, Captain Cat, thank God, for it was He who brought us here. In fact, if you don't mind, we would love to stay for a while. It would be nice for the children to stay in one place for a bit, instead of continuously moving from place to place."

"Oh, I would be honored to have you stay with me. I don't want to brag, but I think I have one of the most beautiful back-yards in the whole country, and possibly the world, at least if you're like me."

So it was that the Taylor family stayed at the lighthouse for a few years, enjoying every moment with peace and joy. The boys loved the place. They would jump from rock to rock, some-times landing between rocks and just seem to disappear. Other times, they were able to find creatures in the hidden pools from the tide.

The Taylor boys grew very fond of the old lighthouse as the years went by. Jeremy and Victoria were always amazed at how their sons matured, being as young as they were. David was born a leader, and Christopher was born a follower—a follower of Christ.

12

God's Interesting Tool

"Must you really leave? You must understand that there is a storm brewing out there. Anyone would know better than to go out in that storm. You're practically saying that you want to commit suicide!"

"We know that you care for us dearly, Captain. But when the Lord tells you something, it's best to listen and act on it immediately than to think about it for a while, figure out all of the consequences and impossibilities, and then not do it because of fear. 'Perfect love casts out all fear.' Remember that Captain," said Jeremy

"I will. But that still doesn't change the fact that I think this is pretty crazy."

"Yes, we understand that you are concerned about us, and we appreciate that very much. But God said that we MUST GO. I know that there is the possibility that we will die, but I would rather die following Christ through a storm than die on the couch wasting precious time for the LORD. Are you ready, Christopher?"

"Just saying goodbye to so many things that I got attached to over the last six years. Goodbye, lighthouse. Goodbye, pools. Goodbye…"

"How about you, David?"

"Yes, sir. Just getting a book and a pen. I've decided to begin writing a journal. At least for now."

"That's a good idea, son. Hey Christopher, are you done, yet?"

"Just one more. GOODBYE HOME SWEET HOME!"

"We will all miss the lighthouse, Christopher. But I'm sure that God has another special home for us on Earth; and if not, then our next home will be the best Home of all."

"We finally were able to set sail on our magnificent ship, NO FEAR!!" David wrote in his book. *"As we left, it was evident that Mom was missing the lighthouse already, as she clung to Dad as if she would never let go. Christopher, although already eleven years old, began to cry. And me, well, I am a man. At least that's what I told myself. Yes, I shed, like five tears, but THAT was it! We were heading into the unknown. It would probably be our greatest time. Battling the thunder and lightning.*

I couldn't help but yell out a battle cry as we came sailing into the storm. There were fifty-foot waves that crashed over the sides of the boat. What an adventure! 'Hallelujah!' I found myself saying, 'Bring it on Devil! I can handle it with flying colors. I shall stand!' I was thirteen, but I was on fire, and almost literally, as lightning struck the water nearby.

I was in knee-deep water, as the waves crashed over the side of the boat. I suddenly realized that I was a prime target for lightning. I began to think about the best solution for my well-being: 'Run inside where everyone was hiding' or 'Try to bail out all the water with a metal bucket,' but that thought quickly diminished as I realized that lightning was attracted to metal. My only other option was to 'Go down with the ship!'

Many would say that I had horrible parents. I mean, leaving a thirteen-year-old outside on a ship, in the middle of a storm, filled with rain, thunder, and lightning, and I was all alone! That thought may have come to me... like once. I later found out that my father had, indeed, decided to get me, but then God told him to 'trust,' and so my parents left me in God's hands. I honestly didn't care."

Christopher just watched through a window, thinking how crazy and reckless his brother was, maybe even stupid or dumb. Some people might call it bravery, but to him, it seemed that it could be suicidal. And just when it couldn't get worse, it did. Christopher shouted to his parents, "Mom! Dad! David jumped into the water!"

Mom quickly ran to the window. She was shocked. Could this be God's plan to take her son away? Jeremy dashed outside into the rain. He scanned the ferocious waves. Victoria decided to go look at what she had in her first aid kit, in case of any injury—if David were to get back on to the boat. She tried her best to stay calm, but on the inside, she was panicking.

Christopher stood stock still at the window, trying to fig-ure out what on earth was wrong with his brother. Was he attempting suicide? This would be a good way to do it, and that might explain the sudden craziness. Then again, his brother hadn't shown any signs of depression or anything that would make one want to commit suicide. David sure was a mystery, an unsolvable mystery.

Just then, something incredible happened. "Mom! I see David! And he has someone with him!" he quickly told his mom.

David and Jeremy came in and they were carrying a young girl! "Bring her here," commanded Victoria, "Oh dear, by the looks of her wounds, she must have been a slave." After giving some attention to the young girl, probably around the age of ten, Victoria turned to David, who had sat himself down, smiling the biggest smile he could muster, which pretty much meant that he was doing great. "David, are you sure you're ok?"

After he nodded, she again asked, "What on earth would make you just jump into the water like that? You're only thirteen!"

David thought for a little while, then replied, "To be honest with you, I don't have a clue, except that God's hand was in it all. You see, God told me to look into the water where lightning had just struck, and then I thought I saw something shiny, which is odd because there was no light coming through the clouds. Anyway, I decided to just quickly jump in, and not think for a long time about what to do. It didn't take long until my hand touched something solid. I grabbed on, and then prayed to God for a way to get back onto the ship, which I had completely lost track of. The next thing I knew, I was being carried on board by a gentle wave. I'm sorry if I scared you, but God told me to go."

"I understand, but perhaps next time tell us that you are going to jump off a boat."

As the storm continued to rage outside, the Taylor family continued to care for and pray for the little girl that was brought to them.

"Hey, Dad, I'm gonna name every storm from now on. I thought it would be nice to have a name for each storm so that I can refer to it later in my book. Mom, how does King Storm sound?"

"I think the name suits the storm very much. How is the book coming along?"

"Great! This was an excellent idea, Mom."

"You're welcome. I am going to get some food ready. David, how about you stay and watch to see if the girl wakes up? When she does, come and tell me as soon as you can, okay?"

"Okay."

"Jeremy and Christopher, you can go and get some supplies to make a wonderful meal."

Jeremy, couldn't keep back a remark, "Yes, Captain."

Victoria just smiled. As she walked to the kitchen, she wondered what the slave girl's name might be. She looked to be about eleven years old. What had happened to her? How did she get away from her slave ship? And what are they going to do with her? These and many other questions flooded each of the members of the Taylor family as they went about their jobs.

One thing was for sure, King Storm was no ordinary storm. It seemed as though it was leading the ship to where it was to go. It didn't slow down, and it didn't lead the ship to land for many days to come, although it was obvious to the family that there was land nearby because every now and then, they could make out the light from a lighthouse.

About two days after David had jumped into the raging waters of the great and mighty tempest to save the slave girl, she finally woke up. Her wounds were healing quickly, thanks to the tender care of Victoria. The family gathered around, as they wanted to find out the identity of the girl. Jeremy and Victoria sat beside her as tender, loving parents would. Christopher, as usual, was curious and eager to know who his new friend would be. David, on the other hand, sat by the window, watching the storm, while listening in on the conversation at the same time, and sometimes looking at the girl.

Victoria began, "So young one, do you have a name?"

There was silence. Jeremy tried, "Can you understand English?"

She said nothing but just looked out the window near David. Her eyes were transfixed on the ocean around them. No smile was on her face, instead, there was sorrow and worry. Christopher walked close to his brother and nudged him a bit, "I think she's looking at you."

David turned around, his eyes met hers, and it was at this time that David realized why she didn't speak. But at the same time he realized this, he wondered how he realized it because it wasn't obvious—in fact, it was out of this world! He had no idea who she was or what she had gone through, so the only other explanation was that it was from God. "Mom, Dad, I think she's afraid to speak to all of us in the same room. Don't ask me how I know, it's just because that's what God told me."

"Alright. Come on Christopher, let's go outside and enjoy the breeze and some rain."

"Ah, but Mom, I want to listen, too."

"Come on Christopher, listen to your mother."

"Okay, I'm coming."

When David and the girl were alone, she started to look around a little more. She seemed to be surprised, startled, scared, and even joyful, yet there was no smile on her face. She spun in circles and then stopped at a chair and sat down. David came and sat down close by, and then asked, "Do you want to tell me what happened now or not?" She just stared for a long while. "Do you understand English?"

"Only little bit," was the brief reply.

"Well, that's okay. Just share with me whatever you want, I'm ready to listen. Don't worry, I won't hurt you, and I won't tell anyone else unless you want me to."

After a long period of silence and hesitation, the girl spoke, but still wondered whether she could really trust the boy. "Alright. Me try. Me and family go fishing. Big man with whip come, he said he was looking for his cows. We said no see but offered to help. Big mistake. He went with parents one way, and I, with big brother, went other way. We went along beach and then came across big slave ship. We tried to hide, but men see us, and we got surrounded. Big brother try to fight back, but he killed. They took me onboard ship and put to work as slave. Then other man come back with some of my friends, also captured. Mom and Dad not with him."

"We set sail along beach. As we pass by village, we saw village burn down. My parents were trapped in house—it burned down. I start cry. Slave master whip me. Said I no cry no more, or he whip me again. I slave about three years. Name is Kari." When she had finished sharing her story, she bowed her head, ashamed of her past, and yet there was no sign of any emotion, no sadness for her loss, no anger at her slave drivers, no happiness, no peace, and no joy.

Seeing that she probably wasn't in any mood to be talked to at the moment, David just sat there a while, waiting, and wondering how she could hold all of her emotions inside.

"Food is ready!" called Victoria, from the lower deck.

"Do you want to come and eat with us, or should I bring food here for you to eat?"

"I not hungry," was the sharp reply.

"Ah, come on. When you get a bite of Mom's cooking, you're going to be forever hungry. I can guarantee it."

"Fine, but I don't have to talk, right?"

"That's correct. If anyone asks any questions, I'll slit their throats, and throw them off me ship, hahaha. But if you really don't want to come, I can bring food to you here."

"Ok," Kari said. At first, it looked like she was going to stay, but then she changed her mind, "I'm hungry. I go with you and eat food."

David noticed that there was a little different emotion on her face; it was small, but it was something. As David led Kari to meet his family, she seemed hesitant, but at the same time, a bit more secure, as long as David was near.

After supper, Christopher and David put on a clownlike show, which seemed to release the tension and the atmosphere that had encompassed the family and their newfound friend. Kari also began to trust the Taylor family more as the night went on and began to open up to the rest of them.

Before it was time to go to bed, Kari was like one of the family. Each one had their own thoughts as they went to bed. Jeremy and Victoria were, as usual, thinking of where they were headed, what they were going to do with Kari, and what would happen to them next. But in it all, they had peace that God had it all under control. Christopher was joyful in thinking that he had found a new friend or sister. Kari, although she had many mixed emotions, felt at peace, that she was safe, and maybe, just maybe, she would think about accepting that Jesus guy that David had told her about.

Once in bed, she quickly fell asleep. She hadn't felt such a soft bed in a long time. David stayed watch outside for a while before going to sleep. He was satisfied with how the day had ended. He knew that the tempest and any hardships that would come their way would just be interesting tools to guide the Taylor family on their way. David didn't know what would happen next, but he knew that God would provide the peace, joy, and patience to get through every tribulation. He was ready to rise up to the higher calling that God had in store for him.

13

"Why?"

"Land Ahoy!"

"Let me see, David. Well, you are right about that. Since it's early morning, we can look around to see what the land is like before we make any official plans to stay for a while or not."

"Hey Dad, what do you think we will meet on this land?"

"I don't know, but whatever we meet, I trust that God has a perfect plan. Even though we don't always know why He does the things He does, the way He does."

"Like with Kari, Christopher, and Mom?"

"Yes, exactly. That is always the hardest part. When a loved one leaves or dies, and you feel like you really need them, you ask God to bring them back; but He has a different plan in mind, and we don't know how it will all turn out. It sure is hard to have peace in those times and even harder to have joy in it all, but you have surprised me. You have been joyful during times that I felt like cursing God, but seeing you helped me realize that I had to have faith and trust that this was the better way."

When the two had finally reached land, they began to look around. The ocean breeze was steady. In the great distance, the cliffs stretched out their heights to the heavens. Rocks dotted the shoreline as the sand on the beach rolled toward the jungles that swayed steadily up to the mountains behind them.

Just as the two were about to head into the deep jungles, they heard a racket beyond the rocks that surrounded them. They crept up slowly, not wanting to attract any unwanted attention. As they peeked over the edge, they saw two natives fighting, one had a spear, and the other had a knife. The one who had the spear had a few cuts already and looked to be a younger man than the other. The older one had so many tattoos and face paints that it was difficult to see what his face actually looked like. David and Jeremy guessed that the younger had done something wrong or had challenged the elder for leadership. Either way, it looked as though they were fighting to the death if no one stopped them.

"Dad. What do we do? We must do something! We can't just let them kill each other off. That's not what God wants."

"I know, son. Alright, let's make a dash for it. You take the younger, and I'll take the elder. If we can stop them from using their weapons, then we should be able to get the upper hand. Ready? On 3—1 . . . 2 . . . 3!"

The two dashed across the shoreline, like pronghorns running from a cheetah. Just as the elder was about to give the finishing blow, Jeremy bulldozed over him. The younger just stared, not sure what to think, but then grabbed for his spear that was nearby and tried to strike the white man who was intruding on their turf. But instead of having the full reach with his arm, it was held back by another white man.

The older man, although temporarily stunned, looked around for his knife. Just as he spotted it, Jeremy jumped on top of the knife, so that the native couldn't pick it up. The older man became angry that his precious knife was being stepped on and retaliated with a punch to the stomach, which knocked Jeremy on his back.

"Dad!" David yelled and took his opponent's spear from him and whacked it over the elder's head, causing it to bleed. David was just about to finish the job, but then remembered that God would certainly not be pleased with him if he did so. In response, David knelt in humbleness and asked for forgiveness for the wrong that he had committed.

Jeremy, although still shaken from the blow to his stomach, acknowledged his mistake also as he looked toward his son and kneeled, even though he knew that the natives would probably kill them as soon as they retrieved their weapons.

"S'tah ghuone!" boomed a voice from farther away. The natives lowered their weapons and bowed as the chief came walking past. He walked around the kneeling white men and then spoke in his native language to his men.

Jeremy and David, after finishing their prayers, looked around, surprised that they were still alive. They were even more shocked by the increased number of natives that surrounded them. One stood out in particular and was obviously the chief.

Another man, much smaller than the chief, came and kneeled close to the two missionaries and spoke in their language, "You come with us. You fulfilled prophecy. Prophecy say, 'Kneeling white men come to land and save native'. Native not kill you."

As the months moved slowly by, Jeremy and David began to let go of their homes, and the families and family members that they had to leave behind, and they began to see their new home full of laughter and joy. Full of gifts and struggles, but it was becoming home.

It took the two a while before they were able to understand the natives' language, and it was only then that they were able to fully understand the prophecy that saved their lives.

Long ago, there was a war that cost the natives their previous home, and almost all of their lives. Near the end of the war, there was a native that had been meditating, and it was then that he was given a vision—a vision of two white men kneeling.

The vision also showed that the two were the key to victory over their enemy after many, many feasts and festivals were held. It was then that the chief of that time decided to flee the battle in search of a new home and the two white men.

Jeremy and David constantly told the natives that they were not warriors, but they knew someone that could save their lives, and more importantly, their souls. So, the two shared stories of the great King and His Son, and many believed and were saved.

Jeremy, now at the age of thirty-nine, knew that it was time for him to slow down as his short, but dangerous and adventurous life had caught up to him and had begun to break down his body, but his spirit was as strong as the day he knew who he was meant to be.

It was this same spirit that Jeremy pressed daily on his son. With the help of his Dad, pushing him on in life spiritually, physically, and mentally, he excelled in whatever he did, especially in the realm of leadership and storytelling.

In fact, it was on a particularly special day the chief decided that, for his daughter's birthday, he would ask young David to tell them the story of how they got to the village since he had been told that it was a story of adventure and danger.

So, everybody young and old, in fact, the entire village, came to surround the young man as he told them about the hard journey he and his father had taken to get to the village. It was soon discovered that the story would take a little longer than a night to tell; so early the next morning, just before the sun came out, the storyteller continued his story, as he did for the following days, every morning, and every night.

"Land Ahoy!"

"Are you sure, David? Because you've said that like a hundred times already."

"This time I'm serious. You can come up yourself if you like."

"We hardly have enough space up there."

"It's not that high up, unless you're scared, Christopher."

"Fine, I'll come up."

Christopher climbed up the ladder to the lookout. Then, just as Christopher was almost at the top, David yelled at the top of his lungs, "Canon ball!!"

Splash!

Water splashed over the sides of the boat where Jeremy and his wife were relaxing. Jeremy and Victoria jumped awake as the water soaked them through.

"David Taylor! Why on earth would you do such a thing? You almost gave us a heart attack!"

"Same here," Christopher said, as he climbed down from the lookout.

"There's land up ahead! And I'm not joking around this time."

"I saw it, too."

"Alright then, climb on board. Let's sail straight for the shore," said Victoria.

The family reached land on June 23, 1844, and as it was just after midway, David and Christopher went to fetch some sticks to build a fire, and Victoria went to look for food. Jeremy looked for a place to set up camp.

"Hey, David, you know that I'm not the biggest fan of the ocean, like you and daddy, but I felt much safer on that little raft than I do in this dark jungle."

"You know Christopher, I didn't always love the big waves and the thunderstorms. I was quite scared of them. And believe it or not, I still am."

"Well, if you really are telling the truth, you sure don't act like it."

"You see, Christopher, this is how it works. Whenever I get scared, I am reminded that God is always with me. And if he is always with me, then how can I be afraid of any giant wave? I always recall the same Scripture that Mom and Dad always talk about, Jeremiah 29:11. 'For I know the plans I have for you,' declares the LORD, 'plans to prosper you, and not to harm you, plans to give you a hope and a future.' And when you really think about it, the same God who controls the whole universe, even the smallest creature, is by my side. Fear just doesn't stand a chance, and the only direction it can go is away from me. 'Resist the enemy, and he shall flee.' Fear is our enemy, Christopher."

"Huh. I never thought of it that way before. Thanks, David, you really are the best brother I could ever ask for."

"You're welcome. I think we have enough sticks for the fire, let's go back."

"Okay."

____

As the moon shone brightly that night, and the stars twinkled, the family went to sleep, except for Jeremy, who decided to stay watch for a while. As Jeremy stayed up watching the stars, he recalled the tragic event that had befallen them soon after King Storm had dispersed into thin air.

____

It was a sunny morning, the first one they had seen in twenty days. In fact, it was the first time since they'd left the lighthouse and Captain Cat. They would have lost track of the days of stormy weather had it not been for the fact that David watched the skies super closely, so he was able to recognize the change in lighting, even though it was so rainy and cloudy that the sun, moon, and stars could not be seen. He numbered each day in his journaling book.

"Life is that way. Many times, our struggles, addictions, sins, and many other problems we face cloud over our lives so much that it seems God is so far away we can't see him," wrote David in his journal

one morning. *"But His light is always shining, and just as I have kept watching, waiting, and hoping for the sign of a new day, we too must watch because all it takes is a little light to fill all of our needs. Darkness cannot stay where there is light. And where there is light, there is always a source. Darkness has no source, so it must leave when the light comes in. It can only reign where the source is cut off, and we have the power to switch the light on or off."*

During the next two months that they spent together with Kari, they went through some interesting times. There were times of laughter, times of sadness, times of anger, and of hurt. Yes, there were some real good times and some real bad times, but together, they pulled through it all.

The family's favorite time was during story time. David was, by far, the best storyteller because he gave great attention to detail in everything. And as Kari told her stories, everyone listened attentively as these stories were stories of her past, such as the times she was a kid. These were tales of joyful times, though they were often followed by the tale of her enslavement.

Oh, the anger and hurt that was evident in Kari's heart. It broke the Taylors' hearts to hear of all the things that Kari had dreamed in her heart to do to the man that had shown her undeserved cruelty. Their souls wept for her lost soul. Oh, what a glorious warrior she could be for the Lord, but she didn't want another master. She wanted to rule her own life and be her own master. The Taylors' attempts to bring her to know Jesus were futile.

So, they decided that the best thing they could do for her was the simple but many times challenging thing of being a bright and shining light to her. So, they gave her to the Lord and let Him touch her heart. It was the only way to truly reach her.

Then, one cloudy morning, it looked as though perhaps their prayers might have finally broken through the enemy's cloud of darkness.

"David, can I ask you a question?"

"Sure. Go ahead, Kari."

"How can you be so joyful and forgiving all the time? I mean, just the other day, Christopher poured boiling hot water on you. I mean, at first, it looked like you were going to lay it all on him. But then you just pushed it all away, the pain and anger, and you forgave him. How?"

"Well, I think you already know the answer to that, but it's not always easy. Besides, it was just an accident, nothing intentional."

"Yes. But how would you react if you were in my situation?"

"I honestly don't know. My Dad would know better. You should ask him."

"Really? Did he get whipped, too?"

"Not exactly, but he did struggle with some of the same feelings you do. How about you ask him after supper today?"

"Okay."

Just as supper was finishing up, David said, "Dad, Kari has a question for you."

"Well, then fire away."

"Well, sir. David told me that you might have gone through something hard like me, and had had the same feelings I do now…"

"What are you referring to, Kari?"

"Dad," David replied for Kari, "I was thinking of the incident that occurred when you were like ten."

"Oooooh, that time. Well, let's clean up the dishes, and then we can go out on the deck for a bit of storytime."

"Alright!!!" Everybody agreed and quickly cleaned things up, and got ready to listen to Jeremy, as he told of a time more than twenty years before.

"Well, Kari, it all started a long time ago. I was about ten years old and lived with my parents. And the neighborhood, well, let's just say it was a blast to spend time with all of the young kids. It was a close-knit village of about thirty families. I had the best of friends. In our group alone, there were about ten kids. We were tied together with tight bonds of friendship. Life was awesome until the war happened.

"Many families left, leaving their lives behind them, hoping that there would be a better life somewhere else, including some of my best friends. You see, life seemed to just drag by with each passing hour. A few of the young men in the village were drafted into the army, and the once-happy streets became gloomy and dark.

"Life was hard. Making a living became hard. I got a job as a paperboy. Warm clothing, food, finance, and health became major issues. My parents fell sick. There was no doctor for nearly fifteen miles. Time passed by, and then, both of my parents died on the same day.

After that happened, I had so many emotions but trained myself not to show them because I had to be the big boy around the house. After the funeral, I heard some families talking about what they were going to do about me. I decided I had had enough of this world. So, I ran back home, took some food along, and decided to hike out, in search of a new life—one that would hopefully be better than the first.

I didn't know which way to go, but I trudged on. Soon, all of my food ran out, and I became really cold, especially after I accidentally fell into a puddle of icy cold water. I had been traveling for approximately a week, without a sign of any house or other traveler. I was alone.

Finally, I entered a town, just as a blizzard caught up to me. It must have been about midnight, for there was no one around and all of the houses were dark. I was out of energy and had begun to think, 'Maybe the time would soon be here for me to die.'

Then, I saw a light. I began to walk toward it, but it was so hard with the wind trying to blow me in all directions. So, I began to crawl, inching my way toward the light. I couldn't see how close I was to the light, but it felt like a few miles. I was so close, yet so far away. I reached out my hand toward the light, but my body was too weak, and I collapsed– unconscious.

The next thing I knew, I was in a huge mansion. Mr. and Mrs. Taylor, along with their three children, had taken me in. It was actually their first-born son that had seen me in the storm and saved my life. Soon, they adopted me, and over the next six years, a lot happened as I received Jesus Christ as my Lord and Savior. I was homeschooled for about four years and grew closer in my walk with the Lord.

It was about this time that I began to question God. I found myself asking several times a day, 'Why did the war have to come? Why did my parents have to die? Why did I have to live?

What purpose did I have on this earth? Why did I have to lose so many of my friends?' But most of all, I asked, 'Why did God make me go through the "fire?"' Many times, when I thought of my original parents, I became angry with God. I blamed him for getting me into this mess that I was in. I became frustrated. I thought I was worthless. I often times thought of suicide. Some might think that's crazy when you have a loving family that earnestly cares for you. But that's what happens when you listen to the lies of the enemy. You think crazy thoughts."

"So, how did you get rid of those thoughts and questions and problems in your life?" asked Kari.

"Well, with some advice from my big brother, Junior, I began to read my Bible; I studied it for long hours, often times past midnight. I also prayed. But the thing that helped the most was this: I realized that God, even though He knows all things, wants to hear from you personally, including how you feel. So, whenever I got angry, I would just simply yell it out at the top of my lungs. Even if it was in the middle of prayer, whether by myself, in front of my family, or even in a crowd, for the closer I drew to the Lord, the less I cared what they thought of me. When I felt sad, I wept before the Almighty King, and He came down to give me a hug. I felt His hugs all the time, and I still do. They are the reason I can go on after every hardship.

"The more I practiced this showing of emotions, the less I felt angry and hateful toward God or anyone that hurt me. I realized that God wants to know the real you, and that includes all the emotions you feel on the inside. You don't need to be perfect to come before Him; in fact, it's especially when you are full of emotions that you need to go to Him. He loves you and that's all that matters."

Silence passed by as each member of the Taylor family hoped and prayed that Kari would realize what she really needed in life was waiting for her. Kari remained silent, contemplating the wise words she had just heard. Eventually, Jeremy decided it was time to go to sleep after he realized that Kari needed some time alone to think, but he made sure that Kari felt free to talk to any one of them if she needed help with something.

Early the next morning, David got up and decided to take a walk around their boat. The story his dad had told last night had been interesting and powerful. He had decided that he also wanted to have those emotional quiet times with his Almighty God. So, he gathered his Bible and journal and prepared himself for a wonderful quiet time, or as he liked to call it, his warrior time.

He examined himself for any extreme emotions so that he could let them out, but to his disappointment, he could only find peace, which was awesome, but he was wishing for something a little louder. "Oh well, I guess it'll just be a peaceful, warrior time," thought David, as he settled down and began to pray.

An hour later, the whole Taylor family began to rise, though Kari hadn't come out of her room yet. Jeremy decided it would probably be best that they leave her alone for now. Time ticked slowly by as the family had breakfast and were now becoming a bit anxious for the girl. "Where was she?"

"I'm going to check up on her. You guys can all stay here," said Victoria.

It didn't take long before she came back, and though everyone was hoping for some good news, it was evident by the expression on her face that it was the opposite. "She's gone!" Worry was etched on Victoria's face.

"What!!!! How can she just be gone?! And where? We're in the middle of the ocean!" Christopher wondered.

"Well, go see for yourself. She's nowhere to be seen."

David and Christopher ran to check Kari's room for any sign that she might have left or maybe a note that told them where she might have gone. Jeremy stayed with his wife, comforting her, and trying to think of why Kari would leave. Soon, the bewildered boys returned. "How could she have just disappeared like that? She didn't even say goodbye." Christopher questioned.

Jeremy, once again not wanting to give up so easily, began to give out orders, "Come on, everyone. Let's not give up hope. Victoria, my dear, can you go see if she might have taken any food from the kitchen? Christopher, go check to see if she took something from the safety box, such as a safety jacket or something. David, can you go out on the lookout and see if you can spot any sign of her? Maybe she's still nearby. We will meet back here in ten minutes."

"Yes, Captain!" the family smirked.

As Jeremy went to see if Kari had maybe left a clue as to where she might have gone, on deck, he couldn't help but wonder if it might have been something that he had said last night that had caused her to leave. He began to worry. Seeing the worried look on his dad's face, David yelled out from the lookout, "Hey, Dad, remember that God gives peace to those who have faith in Him and trust in Him."

"Thanks, son. I really needed that," said Jeremy, as he prayed a quiet prayer. "Father God, please give me peace, so that I might do the work that you have called me to do."

A few minutes later, Jeremy called his family. "Alright, gather around everyone. Let's see what we have discovered about our missing girl. David, are you coming?!"

"Yep. Just hold on a second."

"Alright. So, did any of you find anything?"

"Nope."

"No."

"Well, me neither."

"David, . . ." his voice was cut off.

"Hey, Dad, I think I might see something!!!"

"Where?!"

David quickly climbed down and took them to the spot. "Right here. See? It looks like someone splashed water on here, somehow." The ocean around them was completely calm and quiet.

"That might very well have been her. Good find. But it still doesn't explain what happened to her or whether she's still alive."

After some time, they realized that they might never find out what happened. The family had a moment of silence, while they looked earnestly to God, hoping that once again, His plan was best for them all. As they trusted God, in turn, He granted them peace.

It doesn't mean that it wasn't hard for them, but they were able to pull through it. Kari had become like part of the family to them and not knowing what happened to her was one of the hardest things that had ever happened to them. The hardest thing was not knowing—not only what happened to her, but more importantly not knowing whether she was saved. But that's where faith comes in. They had to have faith and trust in the Lord. That was the only way they could have possibly had peace. But why? Why did God have to take her away, just as they were getting close to reaching her heart? Why did she have to leave? What was God's plan in all of this?

14

Let Go

As hard as it was to let go of Kari, the Taylor family continued to sail south with the constant reminder of land following them on their left side. But God continued to guide them on the ocean currents and gusts of wind.

The lonely nights on the ocean were endless, and even though there were arguments and slight divisions in the family at times, the Taylors could always look up at the great night sky before they fell asleep, and know that God was with them and that He was going to provide for them the necessities of the day. Whether it was food, water, or peace and joy, God would provide it.

This wasn't always easy for the family, to move from place to place; it was often hard to keep moving, especially when they had no idea where they were heading. Many times, they felt lost spiritually and had to remind themselves that God was in control, and He knew what was best for them.

Time had oftentimes become irrelevant, except the position of the sun, moon, and stars, as on the night of June 22, 1844, David noticed that they had changed direction and were heading North, and he also remembered that the sight of a distant land had not come into view for quite some time, which meant that they had come around a southern-most point and were now drifting out to sea.

The thought of not making it to land, disheartened David, as much as he loved the ocean, he had started to feel a need for change from their fifteen-month journey. And God having heard his quiet cry, knew they were going to enjoy His next blessing, for He was leading them straight to land!

And sure enough the very next morning, land was in sight, and they were headed right for it. They made it to shore just after the sun reached its peak, and quickly found a good place to build a shelter to sleep the night through.

"Good morning, everyone!"

"Good morning, Dad!" said David, as he just finished building a great and mighty sandcastle. "Hey, Mom, what's for breakfast?"

"Hmmm, what do you think?"

"I think it's going to be fish. You know, even though we've had fish for almost two years now, my tummy just gets excited at the mention of fish for food. I love FISH!!!"

"Well, I'm happy that you like fish, and yes, we are having fish again. But David, you wouldn't have happened to have seen your brother recently, would you? I haven't seen him at all this morning."

"He said he was going to have some intense warrior time. But don't worry, if he doesn't eat his part of the food, I will."

"Hahahaha. I'm sure you would… unless your dad took it before you could even blink."

"No, he wouldn't."

"I might."

"No!"

"Yes!"

Before the argument could continue, Christopher came tumbling out of the jungle. He had the biggest smile on his face—bigger than he'd had in a long time. "So, Christopher, are you going to explain to us why that big, curved line is stretched across your face?" asked Jeremy.

Christopher replied with a sharp but cute, "No." And that was all the family was able to get out of him. Even during breakfast, Christopher kept smiling. It was like he had this huge scheme that he was planning to prank his brother with, but that couldn't be it either because Christopher was not a trickster. Maybe it was just something the Lord told him that he really needed, I mean, he'd spent approximately two hours with the Lord that morning, so something must have been up.

As David and Victoria cleaned up, Jeremy and Christopher took a stroll across the wide sandy beach. "Mom, what would happen if God decided to take one of us home? How could we cope with that? I mean, sure, we lost Kari, but if someone, let's say, Dad, would leave, how would we survive without him?"

"I don't know, but from what I see, as I look back and remember all that we have gone through together, I know we couldn't have done it without God. I am sure that if He decides to take one of us home, He will bring peace and joy to those that stay."

"Okay. Mom, I know that in this life, we are held alive through God's amazing power, and I know that at any moment, we could be taken home. I just wish I didn't have to die."

"Death is a scary thing, but remember Jesus Christ defeated the grave a long time ago. So, death really should be something that we rejoice in because although death became our punishment when we sinned, God is now glorified, even in death. We as Christians are resurrected in Christ even through death. I know it's hard to be joyful when someone dies, but in Christ, our weakness is made strong. It may be scary, but perfect love casts out all fear."

Thanks, Mom. You're the greatest. I love you."

"I love you too, son."

Both mother and son hugged each other tightly. Half an hour later, Jeremy and Christopher came back. Christopher skipped with joy, and Jeremy seemed like he'd just been defeated in a father-and-son wrestling match.

"David, why don't you go and play with your brother while I have a little talk with your dad, okay?"

"Okay, Mom."

As the boys went to play in the ocean, Jeremy and Victoria sat down on some rocks nearby. "So, what did that little boy of ours tell you? You looked like you had just been through a nightmare when you came walking home."

"I might have. I love how our boys have grown in the Lord so much. Both know His voice, and it's not that I don't believe what Christopher told me, it's just hard to take in."

After a moment of silence, Jeremy continued, "He said that God told him to stay here, alone, as we continue on our trip. He's only thirteen. I know that we have left David alone on the deck of our ship in the middle of the storm, but I can't imagine leaving one of our boys alone with no one to take care of him. I know God is always there, I just wish that there was some easier way, someone that we could trust to care for our boy, you know?"

Silence filled the atmosphere, as Victoria thought about what she was going to say next. But she couldn't help, but think, *"Maybe Christopher understood incorrectly, or maybe there is more to God's plan than they knew at the moment. If they would just wait a bit longer, then maybe God would tell them all to stay."*

Victoria hoped so, as she replied to her husband, "Well, I think the best thing we can do is to pray about it. Let's do that now."

Both parents kneeled before their awesome God of impossibilities, asking what they should do. They prayed for a long time, but there was no answer. Silence filled the atmosphere. The boys had stopped playing and just sat down on the sand with the waves lapping at their toes. The only sounds were the crashing waves and birds chirping, with the occasional lemur in the distance.

Then, suddenly, the two boys dashed along the sea heading toward the jungle that was further inland. Jeremy and Victoria wondered where they were going and decided to follow behind quickly, trying to catch up to them while calling out their names. Over fallen trees, around rocks, through bushes, and under vines, the boys dashed this way and that way, while their parents had a hard time keeping up.

Soon the boys stopped, and what was before them was the most beautiful thing they had ever seen. Even their parents couldn't believe what they were seeing, as their mouths began to fall to the ground in awe of the splendor that was before them.

Oh! How wonderful! How beautiful! How awesome was the Lord's Creation! The family was looking over a cliff's edge and not far away from them was a gigantic waterfall pouring down hundreds of gallons of water per minute. The water crashed down to the bottom as it hit a pool of crystal-clear water with a colossal splash! From the pool, the water swirled round and round, flowing through tunnels carved through small hills or around huge rocks. There were so many fruit trees along the banks of the river. The entire valley was covered in green grass and trees.

And way in the distance, Christopher noticed that there was a small hut and possibly a garden. "Hey, look over there. Who do you think lives there?"

"I don't know, Christopher. We will go look there as soon as you answer this question. How did you find this place?" asked Victoria.

"Oh, that was easy. We just followed the little stream that runs from the waterfall, through the jungle, to the beach. Christopher spotted it first. See, there it is!" explained David, as he pointed toward the little stream.

"How did we not see that before?" questioned Jeremy. "Anyway, just as we promised, let's go down and see who lives here, but be careful, there could be dangerous animals around every corner, or maybe whoever lives here isn't friendly."

The family slowly walked down a path from the clifftop to the bottom of the waterfall. The air was so fresh, so relaxing, and so... so fulfilling. Birds flew by in flocks, and the butterflies fluttered up from the ground. There were flowers of all kinds, roses, tulips, and orchids. God's music filled the air as the birds harmonized, woodpeckers drummed on the trees, the bees hummed, and the lemurs howled with a loud bass sound not far in the distance. It was evident that Victoria was in love with this place. She went swirling among the tall grass, living the life of her childhood once again.

As the boys ran ahead chasing the butterflies, Jeremy spoke quietly to Victoria, "This would be a wonderful place to live. There is plenty of food, plenty of fresh water, and so many places to make a shelter to live in." He paused, as a thought just hit him, "Do you think God wants us to stay here a while?"

"Oh, my dear, I would love that, but do you really think this is the end? I mean, I think this might be a short resting place; but maybe, just maybe God wants this to be Christopher's home. Have you thought of that?"

"Well, yes, but I'm still hoping that he might have heard God wrong–or maybe God wants us to stay here with him. But let's wait and see who lives here, then we will pray again, and ask God what we should do."

Just then, the hut came into view. It was more of a treehouse than a hut. Stairs swirled around a massive tree trunk as it rose to the clouds. At the top of the stairs, there was a small porch. The house was made of the most beautiful wood they had ever seen. There was a little chimney at the top of the house from which smoke puffed out. The roof was made of huge leaves bunched together with thick vines and some were covered in blooming flowers.

Christopher, without much thought, ran up the stairs. He was the most excited he had ever been. "Christopher!!" called Jeremy "Be careful! We don't know who lives there." But it was too late. Christopher had popped inside, while David stayed behind at the foot of the stairs. Even he wasn't crazy enough to run into that house. Who knows if there was a native right around the corner with a spear in his hand, ready to impale anyone that came inside?

But soon, Christopher came right back. "It's ok! It's an old, friendly lady!" he shouted down to his family, who were thankful that Christopher was okay. David, however, was still wary. What if it was all a trick, then they would all be goners! But as they entered through the doorway, it was evident that there was no reason to be scared. In fact, it looked as though the lady had been expecting them since she had a giant pot of soup over the fire and had also made a huge pitcher of juice. Or maybe she was expecting someone else to come?

"Welcome, my friends! Please, come and have a seat. Don't worry, I won't bite unless you bite first," the old lady said. As everyone found their seats in the little house, the old lady said, "You know, I've been expecting you."

This shocked the entire family, as they wondered who she was and how on earth was she expecting them. "Oh, where are my manners? I'm sorry. My name is Ziporah. I am an assistant keeper of this wonderful creation that is before us. You are welcome to take food from everything that you see here. For what's mine is my Master's, and what He gives me, I give to you."

"So, you're not going to eat us?" asked a nervous David.

"What?! No! How on earth could you think something like that of me?! Oh... I understand you think that since I am a native, I'm a cannibal. Well, young man, I'll have you know that I am quite the opposite of a cannibal."

"Sorry, ma'am."

"That's okay. And please, call me Ziporah, or Zip for short. Now, I know you all have several questions, although only some might be for me. So, go on and ask me. Get on with it."

"Well, if you don't mind . . ." Jeremy began but was interrupted by Ziporah.

"I don't mind. Sorry, go on, Jeremy."

Jeremy was surprised, "How did you know my name?"

"Oh, so it is your name. Well, if that one is true, then your wife's name is Victoria the Colorful and Wise Youth, and your sons' names are Christopher the Obedient and Patient Traveler, and David the Chief, the Joyful Wise Warrior. And you, my young man, are Jeremy the Peaceful Peacemaker. Did I say that already? I'm sorry, I guess I might be getting on in years. The old mind isn't working as well as it used to."

After a moment of silence, during which Ziporah enjoyed the wonder and awe of her guests, she continued. "And in answer to your question about how I know all your names, Peacemaker, and your question about the titles, Warrior, I saw it all in a vision from the Creator. I know Him just as you do. And I know that from a vision, as well," chuckled Ziporah. "Come let me show you, your rooms. You can ask questions later. Now, it is time to get some rest."

The Taylor family followed Ziporah to their rooms. They had so many questions about this lady who seemed to know more about them than they knew about themselves. They had so many questions, many of which were answered in the next few days.

Christopher learned to enjoy this place more every day. Then after having stayed for almost a week, during his quiet time, the Lord spoke to him. So, he went to his parents with this remark, "Mom, Dad, I believe God wants me to stay here with Zip." Knowing that his parents would once again think about it, he ran off. He wondered why his parents wouldn't let him stay; God had called him, and God would take care of him.

Jeremy and Victoria were once again faced with a seemingly awful decision. What were they to do? How could they leave their son on an island full of dangers? How could they just leave him, knowing they might never see him again?

Both parents decided that they would go talk to Ziporah, as she seemed to know the answer to almost everything. They found the old lady sitting on a log near the bottom of the waterfall. Christopher was sitting beside her. To him, she was like another grandmother.

"Hey, Christopher, can we talk to Ziporah alone for a moment?"

"Sure, Dad."

After the two were comfortably seated on the log, Zip asked, "So what seems to be the problem with you two? You look like you've seen a ghost or something."

"Well, Ziporah, we were wondering if you could give us some advice concerning Christopher."

"Hmmmmm, would it have anything to do with the decision of leaving Christopher here with me, and you two continuing on sailing to wherever God leads you with David?"

"How did you know? Did God tell you that in a vision?"

"No, but I wish He had. I like those visions very much. Anyway, in order to answer that question, Peacemaker, Christopher told me all about it already."

"Ok. So how would you respond to that? I mean, how can a parent that truly loves his or her child simply leave him on an island, knowing they might never see each other again? How is that possible?!"

Ziporah thought long and hard about this question. "That is a tough one alright. Yes, yes yes, that question will require a long moment in the presence of the Lord. Have you already done this?" asked Ziporah as she looked toward Victoria.

"Well, we've just had so many interruptions and distractions that I guess we haven't spent a lot of quiet and focused time with the Lord." She replied while looking at the boys.

Ziporah understood, "Well, then, I'll take care of the two troublemakers, while you go on top of the roof of my house. You'll find a very peaceful place there, and don't come back until you have your answer."

"Thank you, Ziporah," said Jeremy and Victoria as they headed toward the house.

David and Christopher were standing on the riverbank when something crept up behind them. Snap! A stick broke just behind them. As they turned around, they were thrown into the water.

The two boys landed in the water with a great big splash! On the bank, Ziporah lay laughing. David whispered into Christopher's ear, "It's time for some fun!" Then David splashed water onto the bank where Ziporah lay.

"Who did that?!" asked Ziporah.

Christopher pointed toward David.

"Well, then you asked for it." Ziporah quickly climbed on a tree, whose thick branches grew over the river. "Cannonball!!"

A huge tidal wave swept over the boys. They were shocked at the athleticism of the old lady. After the trio got tired of swimming, they went to lie down on a beautiful hill not far from the hut, it was here that they spent the rest of the morning, until their tummies began to rumble. So, they decided to gather some fruits and vegetables from Ziporah's garden for lunch.

As the giant pot of simmering vegetable soup sat over a fire, Jeremy and Victoria finally returned from their quest to find their answer. It was evident that they were both filled to the rim with new everlasting joy from Heaven. "So, did you find what you were looking for?" asked Ziporah.

"Well, not exactly," replied Victoria. "We didn't find what we wanted, but God gave us what we needed; peace and joy, knowing that it would be best if we leave Christopher here with you, Ziporah, while we continue on our journey."

"Really, Mom?! Thank you, soooo much!" Then he stopped dancing for joy. "But that means I have to say goodbye, doesn't it?"

Jeremy nodded, a few tears peaked out from under his eyelids, "But first, let's have this delicious meal and a wonderful, peaceful afternoon before we think on such sad things."

"Wait, what's happening?!" asked a bewildered David, hearing all this for the first time.

"I'll explain later, brother, but can we please eat? I'm dying of excitement!"

A few days later, on a bright sunny day, Jeremy and Victoria prepared to leave. "Well, I think we are all set for sailing," said Jeremy, his face saddened once again at the thought of leaving his youngest son on the isle.

Why did God want to keep his son on the isle? He did not understand, but somehow God's peace was enough to overwhelm him over and over again. That was the only way he could possibly have gotten through this trying time, even though it hurt him so much to have to separate from his youngest son.

The family, including Ziporah who was like a grandma to the boys, met at the dock together one last time. They awkwardly stood around until Ziporah broke the uneasy silence. "Well, if you're not going to say something, then dog pile, hug, or something! Please, don't just stand there!"

With that Jeremy, Victoria, and David wrapped Christopher in their arms. "Oh, we are going to miss you so much, son."

"I'll miss you, too, Dad."

Victoria squeezed even tighter as she spoke, "I love you so, so, soooo much! Never forget that."

"I love you, too. And I promise that I'll never forget," replied Christopher. Turning to David, "Hey, keep an eye on Mom and Dad for me, brother."

"Sure. You know, I always thought that I would be the first to leave the boat, but you beat me to it."

"Actually, Kari beat both of us to that, even though she was our sister for only three months."

"You're right. I'm going to miss you soooooooo much, little brother!"

"Me, too, David! Me, too."

After a few more hugs and kisses, Jeremy, along with his wife and oldest son, David, went aboard their ship, leaving behind another part of their hearts. On shore, Christopher looked out to sea for a long while, and Grandma Zip stood beside him.

Goodbyes are never easy—especially when you know that you won't see the person again, until you die and go to heaven. But somehow, even though the Taylor family had a choice to not follow God's path, and keep the family together, they knew that they would have more joy if they obeyed His voice instead.

15

"Till Death Do Us Part"

"It had been a few months since we had left Christopher," David continued his story for the twelfth day in a row. "We, the Taylor family, Dad, Mom, and I had recently left a pirate ship filled with new, born-again shipmates. Joy had once again been renewed, but that joy seemed to disappear one stormy day. We, as a family, had faced many storms before, but none were as shocking or scary as something became so painfully clear."

Victoria had fallen seriously ill. It wasn't that she was in a lot of pain, but she felt enormously weak. She could hardly walk fifty feet before having to stop and rest.

None of the medicines that were in her first aid kit seemed to help. Jeremy prayed for healing and a miracle all day long, but none of it seemed to help. David stayed watch outside, hoping to spot land or maybe another ship. But day after day, there was nothing but the deep blue sea.

Then one sunny morning, David finally spotted something in the distance. He pulled out his telescope that a converted slave captain had given him.

"Dad! Dad! There's a ship that's heading our way!"

"I'm coming! I'm coming!"

Sure enough, there was a ship sailing toward them. It was evident that the ship was a big one, and it was not a pirate ship either. Minutes later, the two ships made contact. The bigger one put down ladders for the Taylor family, David climbed up, while Jeremy stayed with his wife. When David returned from meeting with the captain of the ship, his face was beaming with delight.

"Dad, they are friendly, and they have a professional doctor on board who would be glad to offer his services for Mom!"

"That's awesome news, son. Bring him aboard."

Jeremy and David waited outside as the doctor examined Victoria. They didn't mind too much because it gave them a chance to minister to the sailors.

The doctor was in the room with Victoria for a long time. A few times, Jeremy had enough of waiting, but David reminded him to trust in the Lord, and it would be okay.

Finally, the doctor came out and asked the rest of the family to enter the room. Jeremy and David had just finished praying with some of the men. As they passed by the doctor, who was holding the door open for them, they noticed that he had been crying. But why? Jeremy went to sit by his wife's side, and David stood close by.

"I have some good news and some bad news," the doctor began. "The bad news is, well, it's actually really bad." A short moment of silence followed before the doctor continued, "your wife, sir, has a disease that is incurable. I am sorry, but your wife has cancer."

David was shocked as the news was relayed, and Jeremy was almost pale—but Victoria was at peace in her heart.

As the words that were spoken sunk in, the family began to weep for Victoria, for she was practically sentenced to death unless their loving Father had the desire to heal her with His miraculous power.

After a long, long time, David spoke up, since he had noticed that the doctor was still in the room. "So, what's the good news then?"

"Well, the example that you have all shown has moved me to believe that there really is a gentle, loving Father up there in Heaven. I have accepted Him as my Savior and have made Him Lord over my life. Thank you so much for showing me His peace and joy. I have been searching for those two things for twenty-seven years, and now I have them. Thank you so, so much."

The next day, it was time for the ship to continue its journey. The doctor left some medicines and pills to lessen the pain. He was sorry that he couldn't do more.

As both ships waved goodbye to their new-found friends, the doctor called out, "Thank you, again, for the peace and joy that you helped me find. I pray that you will have both as you continue with your travels, and I also pray for a miracle. May God bless you, and I hope to see you again. Goodbye friends, and farewell!"

After the ship left, time continued to drag by, and Victoria continued to get worse. But even with illness, there was peace in her heart. "'For I know the plans I have for you,' declares the LORD. 'Plans to prosper you, and not to harm you. Plans to give you a hope and a future,'" she would often remind both men that stood beside her every day.

Jeremy continued to pray for her, day and night. Sleep was drained from his soul. David wasn't much better off. The thought of losing his mother at the age of sixteen wreaked havoc on his poor soul. Sometimes he wouldn't eat for days. He tried to keep his mind busy with other stuff, such as keeping a lookout, cleaning the ship, guiding the ship, or sometimes even cooking.

Then one night, as David had his devotions out on the deck, he heard the Lord speak something to him. The voice was as clear as thunder, in fact, it sounded like thunder. It sounded as though it came from a fog that seemed to have been following them since they'd left Christopher on the isle.

The Lord told David, "DAVID TAYLOR, CONTINUE TO PRAY FOR HEALING FOR YOUR MOTHER! DO NOT GIVE UP!"

David jumped up. He was completely shocked. *"The Lord wants to heal my mom!"* thought David. *"I have to go tell Dad!"*

When Jeremy heard the news, although he was happy about it, he was obviously tired and weary. He couldn't help but think, *"But that's what I've been doing all along. Why will this be any different? Why hasn't He moved in healing my wife already?"*

It was as he thought this that the Lord reminded him of who He really is—Love. The Lord brought to Jeremy's mind several verses:

Galatians 6:9, "And let us not be weary in well doing; for in due season we shall reap if we faint not."

Hebrews 12:1, "Therefore, since we are surrounded by such a great cloud of witnesses, let us throw off everything that hinders and the sin that so easily entangles. And let us run with perseverance the race marked out for us."

James 1:3, "because you know that the testing of your faith produces perseverance."

And James 5:11, "As you know, we count as blessed those who have persevered. You have heard of Job's perseverance and have seen what the Lord finally brought about. The Lord is full of compassion and mercy."

"Thank you, Father, for Your Word," replied Jeremy.

Over the next few weeks, Jeremy and David poured out their hearts in prayer. David especially, since he had heard God say that he was going to heal his mom—at least he was fairly sure of it.

But the more they prayed, the worse Victoria became. One day, Jeremy had had as much as he could take as he questioned, "Why, God?! Why must it be this way?!"

David had also questioned this several times, but he always quenched the thought by telling himself, "God must be planning a huge miracle." So, he prayed harder.

Soon, Victoria got so bad that she couldn't even sit up. Her voice became quiet and shaky. It became quite evident that she probably didn't have a lot of time left.

One day, she called Jeremy by ringing a little bell that was beside her, and she told him to bring David in. When they both returned, she hugged each one and then began to speak in a hushed voice, "I believe that God is calling me Home. I know that you have been praying so much for healing so that I might be able to go on many more adventures with you, but my prayer has always been that you will not be angry at God if He decides to take me Home, anyway. And if He does decide to take me, you might never know why; but from what I have seen, you both have grown so much in your relationship with the Lord. Promise me that you won't give that up."

"We promise."

"Good."

16

Change

"A few days later my mother died," ended David, tears rolling down his cheeks as he told the story to the natives who paid close attention. "She had lived a youthful and victorious life. My father could tell you more about her life than I ever could, I'm sure of that. But that story may be for another time. I still don't understand why God had to take her from us, even though I am sure that He had promised healing. But maybe I was wrong. Maybe when I heard God say that He wanted me to pray for her, my mind readily jumped to the conclusion that my mother was going to be healed. Human minds tend to do that. We, many times, assume something just because that's what we want to hear. I do hope that our story has also helped each one of you in your lives, even though it seems as though it was a mess—it was a fruitful mess."

"Mista David," asked a little boy, "where did you bury ya Mum?"

"Well, it was Mother's wish that we put her body into the sea. That might sound crazy, but it's true. She was born on the ocean, on a small sailboat, so she wished to be buried in the sea too."

"That sound cool! I want to be buried in the sea, too," the boy replied.

"Okay," David stopped and thought a little bit. "From this story, I really hope that you can learn some life lessons. I think one of the important ones is that you are never too young to do God's will. One can see this, as we look back, and see when each of our family found their purpose in God. My father, Jeremy Taylor, was called to become a missionary at age fifteen and set out on his own voyage at the age of sixteen. Christopher found his at fourteen when he stayed on the isle. My mother, according to my father, found her purpose at twenty-two. And me, well, I think I've found mine here with you, at age seventeen, when we landed here about half a year ago."

"Does that mean you'll stay here with us?" asked another little one.

"For now, yes. But if God calls me away, then I will go. Until then, we shall stay."

Three years later, Jeremy and David still lived in the little village. All the elders, along with most of the rest of the village, had already received Jesus Christ as their Savior. And most of those had made Him Lord of their lives.

Jeremy, although he was only forty-two, was a grandfather to all the children in the village. David, now almost twenty, grew in unmatchable wisdom every day. He also excelled as a warrior.

It was a lovely day in the village, and David was just finishing up a story of either his, or his family's travels, or a Bible story to the little ones, as he did every month.

The elders had gathered to discuss some important matters. They stopped to watch David for a moment. At the end of the story, a little boy asked David, "So what happen to fog?"

"Well, when my mother died, it seemed to have slowed down, for it drew farther and farther away. Sometimes, I thought I saw a ship in the fog, but I believe I had just been out at sea for far too long. Sometimes, however, when I wake up really early and go out to the lookout cliff, I think I still see the fog far off in the distance."

"Really?"

"Yep."

"Wow. That's cool... and creepy."

After answering all of the questions and dismissing the little ones to go play, David went to search for Zara, the Chief's daughter, and the woman of his dreams. She had long dark hair that reached down to her waist, and her eyes sparkled as if they were jewels. To David, she looked like an angel, as she tended to those that were in need. Whether it was the old or the young, she was ready to serve with patience, peace, and everlasting joy.

The elders watched David leave. One of the chief's closest friends spoke up, "The young David is such a blessing to us. He is wise, strong, loving, kind, forgiving, always at peace, and full of joy."

"He is also handsome," said another. "I think he would make a wonderful husband and son-in-law—and perhaps a chief. What do you think, Jagat?"

Just then, a scout came dashing in. "Sir . . ." he panted as he tried to get enough air in his lungs. "I saw . . . I saw seven fires."

"Do you know whose ships they are?" asked the chief.

"Yes, sir. The bonfire was lit shortly after the seventh fire. They are Warinder's fleet!"

17

The Drums of War

Everyone gasped. Surely now it was time to prepare for war. The chief called another messenger to go beat the war drums.

Warinder was a tyrant at heart. He was the meanest man to sail the Atlantic, Indian, and Pacific Oceans. He was ruthless and cruel, a slave captain and pirate. He murdered needlessly, often burning people in their own houses. Many of the villagers called him "hellfire" or "the devil's executor." He believed that mercy, joy, peace, and love were all signs of weakness, and he ensured that all of his men knew that well.

Warinder had the biggest fleet of ships known to all islands. There was normally only one option when the tyrant came to your village—flee for your life as fast as you can! But maybe this time there was another option—now that they knew the Lord Almighty as their God.

David joined the men of war at the Table of Strategies, where war plans were made. Many ideas were presented to the chief, none of which gave him peace of success.

After about an hour of chattering, everyone quieted down and went home, after the chief dismissed them, and he said that he would present them an answer in the next three days.

The following night, Jeremy and David ate supper at the chief's house. After the meal, the chief began to speak to David about the upcoming war and whether they should fight or flee. "What are your thoughts? I ask because none of the other ideas gave me peace about the situation, but you always seem to have an excellent answer when others don't."

"Well, when I was young, I had always dreamed of fighting with spears and swords and such, but God has given me a different idea of war, one that actually gives me peace. However, I know that some men would disagree with me, and I do not want to start a war among the people when that is not the real battle that we are facing.

You see, Chief, God reminded me of a story in the Bible. Do you remember the story of Jehoshaphat and the Three Armies? Jehoshaphat realized that the battle that was coming to him was much bigger than he and his army could handle. So, he went to God and prayed to the Almighty Creator. God answered through another man, saying that Jehoshaphat didn't need to worry about fighting this battle because God was going to fight the battle. All they had to do was to go and face the battle, but they would not have to fight it. I believe that's what God wants us to do. I believe he wants us to face the enemy and watch him come crashing down, without us doing anything."

"You mean, you want my men to just sit and watch?!"

"No, I believe that God wants your men to prepare their hearts. Instead of preparing weapons of physical war, let's prepare for spiritual warfare by fasting and praying until the battle comes. I suggest that the women and children be moved farther inland, about a mile or two, so that if anything does go wrong, they won't be in harm's way. And during the time that we watch victory fall into our hands, we rescue the slaves and free them. We give them proper clothing, food, and water, and throw a party for them after the war is over.

During the battle, I would insist that no one retaliates in any sort of way. Let the enemy run out of their own weapons. If God allows some to survive, and they surrender, we shall be kind to them, just as we will be kind to the slaves. This may even include Warinder—we must be kind to him too. God is the Judge, and we are not, therefore it is not our job to judge him unto death. Remember, the Bible says that we should 'be kind to those that hurt us and pray for those that persecute us'."

After a moment of silence, the chief said, "You know, as crazy as that plan sounds, it is the only plan that has given me any pinch of peace, even though my flesh thinks it's the worst plan I've ever heard. Thank you for sharing with me. Your wisdom and advice are much appreciated in our village."

"Thank you, sir. But remember, we must really be thanking God for this wonderful plan of His."

After three days, Chief Tarak shared the war plan, and as expected, it was evident that there were some that didn't agree; but many others, although unsure of the plan, trusted in their chief's decisions. He was hardly wrong, and even more so since the two white men entered their village and talked about the greatest Leader of all time.

In order to help the warriors and their families understand why the chief had decided to take such a strange form of battle, David spoke before the entire village. He retold the story of Jehoshaphat from his worn-out Bible. He, along with his father, had been working on translating the Bible into their native language, though several had learned quite a bit of English during the years that Jeremy and David had lived in the village. They had already completed the first Gospel.

After the story, everyone went to eat lunch as they contemplated what was said. That afternoon, David explained what they would do for the rest of the day, and for the time they had left before Warinder's fleet would be in sight. So, the rest of the day was spent gathering food, and first aid kits, and making sure that they would have enough food for a feast after the war. The following day, and for several days after, everyone in the village began to fast and pray. They began seeking the Lord with all of their hearts, souls, and minds. Even though many did not have a Bible of their own, Jeremy told them not to worry about it because God knows, so He would meet them in prayer, just as He would when they read from the Bible.

There was one group of men that were half-heartedly praying. Sure, they fasted, just as the others, and they prayed also, but they didn't pray for relationship as the others did. Instead, they prayed for utter and complete victory, which is good too, but better would be a close relationship with the Almighty God, than riches, fame, and praise.

But these men didn't think like that. All they could see was their own selfishness. They wanted to fight a real battle, but they did not realize that the real battle was the one that David and the rest were fighting—the battle of Spiritual forces between God and Devil, between Lord and flesh, and between the one true King and the world.

Five days later, some scouts returned and told Chief Tarak, his advisor, and David, that Warinder's fleet was in sight, about an hour off of their coastline. The drums of war were sounded, as the warriors said goodbye to their families and took up their battle stations. The women and children were led by a band of scouts to their hideout until the war was over.

Jeremy prepared his rescue team, ready to go free the slaves when David signaled them. Most of the men were supercharged with energy, they were rejoicing for the victory to come. It didn't matter that they hadn't had anything to eat for five days— they had fed at God's table.

As they waited at the edge of the jungle near a deep ravine that ran the length of the beach, a mile on each side, until they were cut off by giant cliffs on either side, many noticed that a thick fog had settled down near the edge of the water. Chief Tarak hoped that the fog would not hide the fires that were burning along the beach, to ensure that Warinder would be funneled toward the ravine. David was certain that it was the same fog that he saw every morning when he woke up with the sun. In fact, over the last few weeks, he had noticed that the fog had appeared to come closer every morning, and now it was here, in the middle of the day!

One of the young men asked Chief Tarak, "Sir, do you have anything to say to your people as a word of encouragement?"

"No, but David, do you perhaps have something to say?"

"Yes."

Everyone looked toward David as he spoke, "We must remember the Israelites and their battle against Jericho. Remember, as they marched around the City of Jericho, they were laughed at, but the Israelites kept singing praises to their God and Lord. They marched for seven days, and on the last day, as they were just finishing their march around the city walls, the priests blew their trumpets, and the walls came tumbling down. They praised their God for the victory to come, even though they had a weird strategy. The people of Jericho laughed at the Israelites, but in the end, the Israelites defeated them. Praise is the key to victory in every battle you face."

"May I add something to that?" asked Jeremy. After David nodded, he said, "1 Corinthians 15:57, says 'But thanks be to God! He gives us victory through our Lord Jesus Christ.' And Jeremiah 33:11b says, 'Give thanks to the Lord Almighty, for the Lord is good; His love endures forever,'… 'For I will restore the fortunes of the land as they were before,' says the Lord.'"

"Dad is right," confirmed David. As he looked around at all of the warriors, he noticed that some had fear or anger in their eyes, while others had bravery, wonder, curiosity, and excitement. "In light of these verses, I ask that we don't lose hope in our God. Let us sing praises to our Almighty Lord, as the enemy draws near. 'Do not repay evil for evil, but instead, do good to those that hurt you.' Don't fight back, let the enemy run out of their weapons, and then once they are out, we treat them as we would have wanted to be treated. For it is not our own judging hands that determine the worth of a soul, but it is by grace, and only God's grace, that a soul's true worth may be found. The universe continues to shine forth the glorious wonders of its Creator, the one true Almighty God, Lord, and Savior. Let us give God our glorious sacrifice by allowing Him to fight this battle, for it was never ours but always His. Let Him prove Himself to us; and when we see what a glorious God we serve, what will we be able to do, except praise Him forevermore? Praise Him, warriors! Praise Him! Praise Him!"

18

God's Battle

Just then, Warinder's men crashed through the wall of fog. There were hordes of them; it seemed as though there was an endless number of men streaming through the fog. Jeremy quickly took his men down to the beach and hid behind a ridge of rocks, close to the water's edge.

Chief Tarak stood with his men as they watched the swarms of men come charging over the sand. Jagat, the chief's advisor, stood nearby. Tarak's men waited on the other side of the ravine, which was a few feet higher than the beach.

All of the men were ready to dodge any spears thrown as suggested by David. As they watched the swarms run across the beaches, the warriors broke out in song to the one true King.

Then, suddenly, the ground shook beneath them. Many were forced to sit down, while still others continued to watch the oncoming armies. Then it happened, right from underneath the front line of Warinder's armies—the sand collapsed! Hundreds of men fell down. The sand had collapsed from one end of the beach all the way across to the other side, where a huge landslide of rocks had tumbled down several months ago. There was no way around the gap, which was fifteen feet wide and about thirty feet deep. Water from the ocean rushed through the gap and into the ravine, drowning all of the trapped men that had fallen. Eventually, the gap was filled with enough water and bodies that the rest of the men were able to either climb over their fallen comrades or swim across.

They continued to charge, as they did not see Jeremy run toward one of the ships with his fellow rescuers. The team quickly climbed over the boat's sides. Two of the stronger natives, Veer and Anushka, knocked out the guards. Jeremy then climbed down to the beaten and bareback slaves at the bottom of the ship. There was no emotion as their chains were being loosened for fear that this was all a trick. But instead, the strange white man spoke to them in a calming, peaceful, yet firm, voice as he ordered the natives that had followed him. After orders were given that the slaves were to follow Anushka and some other rescuers, Jeremy, Veer, and the rest of the group continued to release more slaves.

Warinder was a prideful glutton. He wore several headdresses and jewelry from the different chieftains that he had slain. He took great pride in the size of his fleet and in the number of his men, but he had no idea that his slaves were being freed, for the fog was too thick to see through, and he was too busy throwing spears at his new enemy and barking orders at his men, threatening them and whipping their backs to keep pushing forward.

They had now reached a massive ravine that ran between two cliff edges with the beach and the bush tree line on opposite sides of the ravine. The ravine was uncrossable as it was seventy-five feet, at its widest, and fifty feet at its narrowest. The ravine gave all those that fell over the edge a few seconds to self-reflect before a rocky bottom caught their bodies.

Tarak and his men rejoiced as they saw their enemy fall into the Lord's hands. As they shouted out in victory, another great rumble shook the entire land. Kaboom! The ravine widened, making hundreds more of Warinder's men fall, along with a lot of supplies.

Warinder realized that he had already lost half his men and most of their weapons to these amazing wonders. Could it really be true what so many people had said about these natives? Could it be true that the gods of war had abandoned him and had teamed up with these worthless scums? *"It cannot be so,"* he thought, as he drove his men on. *"I have to win, even if it costs me my life. I will always find more men, and I also have lots of slaves to help defeat these natives—if I can make them believe that I will give them their freedom if they fight for me."* But in reality, his slaves were already experiencing the freedom that they had dreamed of since childhood.

Behind the backs of Tarak's warriors, Jagat, the Chief's advisor, was scheming with his friends. He had begun to hate the new advice of this David, as he realized that his job might soon be taken away from him. *And what about this plan of his? It was silly and foolish! How could they possibly win, by just waiting for an invisible God to show up and fight the battle for them? These wonders of land falling were just a natural cause and not of God. In fact, maybe that was David's plan all along, to destroy the whole village by making them believe in an invisible God who fights the battles of His people! What kind of rubbish was that?!*

It would make sense after all. The first day he had met David was on the exact same beach as this one. David had interrupted a battle that was only training, but it seemed that he had planned on killing them both with the help of his father. Probably the reason he hadn't is that he had spotted the rest of the village in the jungle and had just had an idea to kill them all; so, he stopped and knelt down on the sand, and his father followed. Something had to be done, quickly!

David and Tarak rejoiced as they saw the freed slaves come up from behind the village, led by Anushka. David then went to tend to the slaves behind the village, where they would be well out of range of any spear or arrow. Anushka went back to help with more slaves.

Then Jagat had an idea and explained it to the rest of his followers. They agreed to the plan. Jagat went to Ranveer, who excelled in archery, and tried to convince him, "Ranveer, you must hurry and follow me. Take your best archers, come on, we must hurry!" Although confused, Ranveer followed, along with his men. "Ranveer," continued Jagat, "David has sent me to tell you that the plan has changed. He wants you, along with your men, to shoot several fire arrows into the fog, in order to burn the ships, but we must wait for the last slaves to be freed."

"Why would he want to change the plan? It's going great! Don't you see? We are winning!"

"Well, I wouldn't question David's plan. For his plans are always from God, and God never lies. Now hurry, I just saw the last of the slaves leave!"

"I don't think so. If David wanted to change the plan, why didn't he just call me and tell me himself?"

"Are you saying you don't believe the chief's advisor?! I don't know why he didn't tell you himself, but if you don't listen to me right now, a lot of blood is going to be on your head because it will be your fault that God's plan didn't work out. We will lose and many will die because of your selfish reason that David has to tell you himself that the plan has changed!"

After a moment of hesitation, Ranveer ordered, "Alright then men, you heard him, light the arrows. Aim. Fire!" The arrows flew high and far.

Down by the ships, Jeremy and Veer, along with his brother Tanveer, were just getting another ship full of slaves out and into the water. Whoosh! An arrow struck one of the slaves, and he fell dead. Veer looked up and saw that even more arrows were coming. Jeremy hadn't noticed the arrows yet, so when one was coming straight for him, Veer yelled at the top of his lungs, "Move!" as he pushed Jeremy out of the way. The arrow found its mark in Veer's stomach, just missing his spine by a couple of inches. "Aaaah!" he groaned in pain.

Jeremy quickly got up and walked over to Veer. Tanveer ran to his brother's side, "Veer, can you hear me?" Veer nodded. "Come on, let's get out of here," he said, as he lifted his brother up and put his arm around his neck for support. Just then, Anushka climbed over the boat and ran to help. Together, the two of them were able to get him off the ship and into the water. It was then that Anushka asked, "Where's Jeremy?"

"I don't know. I thought he was behind me. Maybe he went ahead to get help."

After the arrows were fired, Jagat ordered his men to spread out and begin to throw spears back at Warinder. The warriors all around Tarak were confused. A few threw spears as they wondered why they were suddenly fighting back—wasn't this supposed to be the Lord's battle?

Warinder noticed that there was confusion among his enemy, and they now had their weapons restocked. *Maybe the gods are on my side after all.* He gave a triumphant yell. Warinder pushed his men onward but soon stopped; he smelled smoke. He looked behind him, and to his horror, he saw that someone had lit his ships on fire! "Retreat! They're burning our ships, men! Retreat!" Warinder turned around and began to run, but not before he threw a well-aimed spear at his target, the chief.

Chief Tarak had had enough of all the confusion and stood up, which he immediately regretted doing. As the spear embedded in his shoulder, he howled in pain. David saw him fall, as he had come to see what was going on. He ran to his chief's side and tried to help him to safety. Jagat pushed him aside and yelled out, "Traitor! You have lied to us. You said that God was going to help us win this battle, instead, you have injured the chief! We should have never trusted you and your God. You tried to deceive us, but you couldn't deceive me. You shall pay for your crimes against our chief."

David was speechless, for he was confused. Jagat had been such a wonderful friend to him for many years. He wanted to say something but decided that it would be best if God defended him. But Jagat's words had stirred up the rest of the warriors.

Just then, Tanveer and Anushka came up the hill, carrying Veer between them. Jagat quickly ordered a bed to be brought for the warrior. He saw another opportunity. "You see, he has even gotten Veer shot, he has betrayed us all. We all know that the penalty for betrayal is death. Death by fire!" All the warriors were getting excited. Jagat was smiling, he had won. "Now, betrayer, what do you have to say for yourself?"

David was quiet for a moment, listening to God. Then he replied in a calm voice. "Let my God defend my name if that is His will, but if not, I shall die knowing that I have done well to serve His all-powerful name."

Just then, Ranveer came stumbling down the hill from where he had been taken by Jagat. He was still carrying his bow, as were his men that were with him. He looked at Tanveer, then Veer. The three were very close brothers. Ranveer was confused and let Tanveer know. Tanveer, who was also having a hard time knowing what was true or false asked, "Ranveer, why did you fire an arrow at the ships? That was not the plan."

"I was told that the plans had changed," replied Ranveer.

"Who told you that?"

"Well, Jagat said that David said that God had changed the plans."

"And that is the truth!" exclaimed Jagat.

"Ok, but what does David say?" asked Tanveer, as he turned toward David.

"Why does it help me to reply, when you still have the decision to listen to Jagat or to me?"

"That is true," agreed Tanveer

Jagat was smiling. His enemy had nothing to say to justify his actions. He was victorious in his plan, and he would lead these people under new leadership when David, the chief, and David's father were all dead.

But Tanveer wasn't finished. "But let us find out who is telling the truth. We shall find out if this God of David's is true or if He is false. Let us see if all of those rumblings and collapsing of the ground from beneath the enemy's feet were all set up or if it was truly by God. May I ask Jagat and all those that follow him, to please come over here and stand here? Then let's bring this traitor and all those that follow him over here." Anushka, Ranveer, Veer, and Tanveer all went to stand beside David. Even the chief, who was losing blood fast, asked that the men carry him to David. Then Tanveer continued, "Now let us ask the God of David, to consume whichever one is in the wrong. If nothing happens by the time the sun is down, then we shall know that his so-called God is false. But if He does respond, then we shall know that He is most definitely true. If He is false, then all those standing alongside David shall be killed also. Do we have an agreement, Jagat?"

Jagat couldn't help but smile. "This was too easy," he thought. For now, everyone would see that this God was false, and they would kill all those that were with this deceiver, including the chief. Then, he would be pronounced the new chief, so he replied, "It's a deal."

So Tanveer prayed, "Dear God, if you truly are God, please show yourself to this village today. Prove yourself before the sun goes down. In Jesus' name, let your will be done."

As soon as Tanveer said "done," the ground opened up beneath Jagat and all of his followers, and it swallowed them up whole, like a snake. But unlike the gap on the beach, it closed up afterward, and there was not a sign that it had opened up.

It was then clear to everyone that the God that David served was the one true God. They began to praise Him for his mighty power, and although they felt a little sad that some of their men, most of them being the elders of the village, had died, they were joyful that God had not killed the man that had shown them how to truly love and how to have true everlasting joy.

Just when they all thought they had seen the greatest miracle of their lives, God surprised them once more. He sent rain to them. It was the first shower they'd had in about two months. But this rain was no ordinary rain, as it was first assumed to be, for it was soon discovered that the rain was cleaning all of their wounds and was healing them completely so that there were no scars—even Tarak and Veer were completely healed.

This truly was a joyful hour, and preparations for a feast began as soon as all of the women and children had safely returned. The Veer brothers, along with their wives, David, and the chief's daughter, and the chief and his wife, went to sit on a hill overlooking the battlefield. It was at that moment, amidst all the tears of joy and laughter, David remembered someone, "Has anyone seen my father?!"

19

Tough Joy

The thought of Jeremy being missing carried away all of the previous joy among these ten. "The last time I remember seeing him was when Veer was struck by the arrow," replied Tanveer. The others shook their heads, except Veer, who seemed like he was trying to remember something.

Then he spoke up, "I think I remember seeing him jump off the boat but on the other side. I wanted to call to him, but I was so dazed by the arrow that I didn't have the strength to call out to him. I don't know where he could have gone," he paused a moment, "Unless . . ."

"Unless what?" asked David.

"Unless he might have gone after a voice that I heard cry out for help. I heard it just before the first arrows were sailing through the fog and into the boats. I'm sorry, David. Maybe if I had really tried to call him, I could have."

"Shhh. It's okay. I don't think he would have listened to you anyway because if I know my dad, he must have felt the Lord tell him to go." David turned to the chief, "Sir, may I send search parties to go look for him? He should be back now. I can't lose him too!" David broke into tears, as the thought of never seeing his father again hit him hard.

"Send as many as you need, son. Ranveer, Tanveer, and Veer, can you each gather anyone available, to go search for our friend? Please bring him home."

"We will search under any rock if necessary. Don't worry David, we'll bring him home," said Tanveer.

The next few days weren't easy for David. As hard as they searched, Jeremy was never found. It was like he had vanished off the face of the earth. With no luck in finding him, many began to think that he might have been captured or killed by Warinder. The search groups continued to search until David decided to call it off. Hoping that his dad would come home on his own.

The whole village mourned the loss of a great friend, father, and grandfather. Many tried to comfort David, as he almost became bitter toward God. He eventually found a cliff edge, where he could look out onto the ocean. One day, a month after David called off the search parties, David sat on the ledge, and as he looked out, he saw fog floating above the calm waters of the deep sea. David felt as though the fog had taken his father along with it, leaving David feeling empty and broken.

Chief Tarak came up beside him and sat down next to David who had sat up at the sound of approaching footsteps. "I hope you don't plan on jumping off."

"No, I was just thinking some things through."

"Look, I know you are grieving for your dad, as it has been about a month since we lost him." He paused for a moment before continuing. "I want to share something with you, which has helped me get through this past year. When I saw that God was truly fighting our battle, and the earth gave way beneath Warinder's army, and when God protected those He loves when Tanveer prayed, my heart rejoiced. I believe that I truly experienced the Father's love, peace, and joy. Sometimes, I doubted that the plan would work, but then God just gave me His peace again. This peace gave me the strength to worship him in the middle of the battle. You see, when I felt the love of God in the middle of the war, I had faith to trust Him that it would be okay. He brought me peace, and once I had that peace, joy filled my heart."

David pondered what was said for a moment, then exclaimed, "So that's the way to true joy. First, one must know that there is someone that truly loves him and would never let him down. Then, the man is able to have faith to trust in the One that loves him. When one truly has trust in another, peace follows close behind. And true joy is only possible when we have peace. Thank you, Chief Tarak. I have been looking for those answers all my life, and now I have them. I just wish that my father was able to hear this." After a slight pause, David realized, "When I really think about it, I've been living what I just said all my life."

"Well son, I must go back to the festivities. We are celebrating all that God did for us, as well as saying goodbye to our friend. I think it is time to heal. I hope you come and join us, and let your brotherhood bless you with their company and wisdom, just as you have shared your wisdom with us. Your father will always be missed, but with God's help, we are able to have joy instead of sadness as we think of him. It won't always be easy, and God never promised that it would be, but He did say that it would be possible. So, we move forward, knowing that there is Someone that loves us so much and who gives His peace and joy to any that ask for it."

"Thank you, Chief Tarak. I will stay and think a little bit more, and then I will join you. Thank you for your words of wisdom, they have already helped me so much."

"Alright, but we will expect your company soon, or we will send out a search party to find you. Haha," joked Tarak, as he returned to his family and friends.

David stayed to thank God for all of the blessings that God had given Him, especially his friends and family. He also asked that God give him peace and joy, as he went down the dark path of losing his parents, brother, and sister for a short while, a grandmother who acted as though she was as young as any other, a Captain with his cat, and a wonderful family back in Iceland. All of these, he might never see again, but that was okay if it meant that God's plan would come to pass. For as the entire village discovered, His plan was always the better plan, no matter how silly or rough it seemed.

As David walked back, he looked toward the future. Although he had lost much in the past, he had gained so much more, which would carry him through the present and the future. Life moved on. There were many challenges the village faced, but there was also much joy through it all.

David and Zara were married the following spring, and David became chief a few months later. Though Tarak, was still only fifty and very able to lead his village to many more great victories, he felt that it was time for David to take the lead. But Tarak knew that he would be there to help David whenever he needed him. This helped David realize that though he had lost an irreplaceable father, he had gained many more that helped fill the void, and they were all in a category of their own.

Under David's direction, the village continued to prosper and flourish. The Veer brothers excelled in every battle strategy, whether it was archery, traps, spears, medical, or protection. God had blessed them, and David, being a wise chief and seeing God's hand on them, moved them up to generals over all of the other warriors.

David prayed every day for his family and friends, hoping that they would be safe, living out the life that God had ordained for them. David knew that he would not have been able to move on if it weren't for the relationship he had with God. God had a plan in all this. Just as His word says, "For God so loved the world that He gave His one and only Son, that whosoever would believe in Him, would not perish but would have everlasting life." David realized that when he looked closer at the verse, the steps to joy were all in that verse. "For God so loved the world that He gave His one and only Son, . . ." showed how much God loved the people that He had created. ". . . that whosoever would believe in Him, . . ." required faith and trust, and ". . . would not perish, but he would have everlasting life" suggested that we would have reason to have peace, for we would not perish, and that was a promise. Instead, we could have joy, for we would live forever in the Lord's Kingdom.

But the promise that David kept closest to his heart was the one that his family shared often with others, "For I know the plans I have for you," declares the Lord. "Plans to prosper you, and not to harm you. Plans to give you a hope and a future." That was perhaps the greatest promise of them all."

About the Author

Jacian Corey Thiessen is a writer who has had a candid interest in writing from a very young age. He is a volleyball player, sports statistician, and author of the new novel, "Joy Amidst Trials".

He was born in Belize, Central America, and resides in the Mennonite community of Spanish Lookout.

Having his roots in a Mennonite community, while at the same time being heavily influenced by the multi-cultural aspect of his church family and country, has created Jacian to be a strong young man of character and open-mindedness. As an author, Jacian strives to bring out the beauty of being different and unique, not tied down to the world's standards, but instead reaching out and testing his own creative mind.

To follow Jacian Thiessen's writing journey check out his Facebook page "Pen of God" and Instagram @writing_for_yeshua_jcnt.

Acknowledgements

It is not enough to say that I, Jacian Thiessen, had a lot of help as I spent much time writing and learning the truths that are shared with you throughout this story. To say that God helped me in every step for the past seven years feels like an understatement, but it's true to every degree and variable. He has provided me with an amazing support team of family and friends. People like my Dad, brothers, and some of my best friends, have helped especially in guiding me with wisdom and truth. I especially want to thank my mentor and great friend, Brent Heveaner, for being there ready to give me guidance and your straightforward opinion on many of the small details of the book, even if some were a little hard to swallow. It would have been a long and much more complicated journey without Brent, and he has helped make this an incredible and awesome journey from start to finish. Many have helped shape me and helped give me the perseverance to pursue and finish strong in my dreams, passions, and my story.

I want to give a huge thanks to Deb Melander who, even while fighting cancer, still helped me greatly in the editing process. The amazing cover was conceived and brought to life by an amazing artist, Karina Dueck.

To thank everybody individually for helping make this dream reach this point, well I might as well spend another year doing so. Even the people that have simply given a notion toward the completion of the book, such as asking how far it had come, or saying that they are excited in anticipation, have helped me to really strive to finish when I felt like quitting.

I will never be able to thank everyone enough for what they did or said to push this project on its way. I am excited to see what God has in store for me and all of the future books that He will guide me to write, as He was and is the true Author of my life, and I am honored to be His Pen. Thank you, Lord, for being you, so that I can truly be me.